THE
DISCHARGE

Gary Reilly

RM P
Running Meter Press
Denver

The Discharge
by Gary Reilly

Published by

Running Meter Press
2509 Xanthia St.
Denver, CO 80238
Publisher@RunningMeterPress.com
720-328-5488

Cover art and book design by Nick Zelinger

ISBN: 978-0-9908666-6-4
Library of Congress Number: 2017933083

First edition, 2017
Printed in the United States of America

Also by Gary Reilly:

The Asphalt Warrior Series:
The Asphalt Warrior
Ticket to Hollywood
The Heart of Darkness Club
Home for the Holidays
Doctor Lovebeads
Dark Night of the Soul
Pickup At Union Statio
Devil's Night

Also:
The Enlisted Men's Club
The Detachment

FOREWORD

The Discharge is the third novel in Gary Reilly's trilogy chronicling the life and times of Private Palmer as he returns from the U.S. Army to civilian life after a tour of duty in Vietnam. It is a largely autobiographical series based on his own two years of service, 1969-1971, which included a year in Southeast Asia.

In the first book, *The Enlisted Men's Club*, Palmer is stationed as an MP trainee at the Presidio in San Francisco, awaiting deployment orders. Palmer is wracked with doubt and anxiety. A tortured relationship with a young lady off base and cheap beer at the EM club offer escape and temporary relief.

The Detachment is the second in the series. This novel covers Palmer's twelve months in Vietnam as a Military Policeman. In the beginning, he endures through drink and drugs and prostitutes but comes to a turning point when he faces his challenges fully sober.

Now, in *The Discharge*, Palmer is back in the United States. But he's adrift. Palmer tries to reconnect with a changed world. From San Francisco to Hollywood to Denver and, finally, behind the wheel of a taxi, Palmer seeks to find his place.

Gary Reilly was a natural and prolific writer. But he lacked the self-promotion gene. His efforts to publish his work were sporadic and perfunctory, at best. When he died in 2011, he left behind upwards of 25 unpublished novels, the Vietnam trilogy being among the first he had written.

Running Meter Press, founded by two of his close friends, has made a mission of bringing Gary's work to print. So far, besides this trilogy, RMP has published eight of ten novels in his *Asphalt Warrior* series. These are the comic tales of a Denver cab driver named Murph, a bohemian philosopher and aficionado of "Gilligan's Island" whose primary mantra is: "Never get involved in lives of my passengers." But, of course, he does exactly that.

Three of the titles in *The Asphalt Warrior* series were finalists for the Colorado Book Award. Two years in a row, Gary's novels were featured as the best fiction of the year on NPR's *Saturday Morning Edition* with Scott Simon. And Gary's second Vietnam novel, *The Detachment*, drew high praise from such fine writers as Ron Carlson, Stewart O'Nan, and John Mort. A book reviewer for Vietnam Veterans of America, David Willson, raved about it, too.

There is a fascinating overlap in the serious story of Private Palmer's return to Denver and the quixotic meanderings of Murph. It is the taxicab. One picks up where the other leaves off. Readers familiar with *The Asphalt Warrior* series will find a satisfying transition in the final chapters of *The Discharge*.

And they will better know Gary Reilly the writer and Gary Reilly the man.

Mike Keefe
April, 2017

PART ONE

CHAPTER 1

One night before the permanent cold of winter set in, it rained. Palmer turned off the lights in the basement apartment and sat near the window smoking cigarettes and looking out at a streetlight reflecting off a layer of water on an olive-colored Dodge which belonged to the man who lived in the apartment on the top floor of the house. His brother Mike had gone out with a friend and would not be back until the bars closed. Palmer was thinking of renting an apartment of his own. His father, who had served in the Solomon Islands in WWII, used to say the one thing he had missed most during the war was to be able to go into a room by himself and shut the door, and Palmer had always understood this on a basic level, but now understood it wholly.

The rain came harder, and he thought of a night in Vietnam when rain flooded the compound, the storm so heavy he had felt safe for once. He put the thought out of his mind because it was a pleasant memory and he refused to attach any nostalgia to that experience. Instead, he thought of a girl he had known before he went off to the war, she was eighteen back then, who met with him after he returned, his first attempt at a date after that year. He felt awkward hugging her, and the few times he kissed her, the gesture seemed dishonest, like the kisses one gives to a prostitute in a puerile attempt to get more than your money's worth. He was upset that he was unable to make a truly emotional contact with her but did not let it show, and when he said good-bye to her he knew he would never see her again and regretted it only on an intellectual level. It was not simple, after a year of intense precaution, to let someone near him, and he smiled it off with the wisdom of an advice columnist who might suggest that, given time, he would readjust. He resented the fact that although he was aware of many changes he had undergone in the war, he had not been aware of this one.

After remaining aloof for weeks, the first night he went drinking with a friend named Mathews, he found himself trying to be the same person he had been when he went away, as if concerned about the possible effects the changes within him might have on the people who had known him before.

The rain slackened and he closed the window shade and turned the lights on.

He had gone out drinking a few times after he got back, and met with men he had known in high school, who had all changed, as he had, some in the war. He felt nothing in common with them, and when Vietnam was mentioned, the only facts revealed were what kind of unit served with and where, and nothing was said, none of the things he was sure they too might have liked to say about the war.

He stopped going to bars. On the occasion that he did end up in a bar, it was across Denver, in neighborhoods unfamiliar to him where he never ran into anyone he knew. He drank alone in his apartment, or with others in their apartments, but with others the point was not to visit but to get drunk. He began experimenting with wines. He had no wish to become a connoisseur, he simply wished to find something palatable and steady, like a weekly TV show which attempts to do nothing more than serve its intended function. Pinot Noir,

Madeira, and an amusing night on Tokay. Worse than motor oil. He found his own level in sweet red wines and looked no further. When he did not want scotch or beer, it was pink chablis, at least two bottles to get him through a night. He drank it by the glassful, with cubed ice, as he was drinking it now.

The rain was like fire crackling on the tin hood of the Dodge, and he pulled the window shut because his bare feet were getting cold.

He had called the house where Celeste's parents lived, hoping she might answer the phone. She had entered the University of Colorado at Boulder the same month he was drafted, and he was hoping she might be home for the weekend, or better yet, had dropped out. No one answered the phone. He took pleasure in fantasizing the misfortunes of people he had once known, and he thought perhaps Celeste had gone away to school, had become liberated at last, and found herself changing diapers with an unfinished degree on her conscience. He would drop by some evening when her husband was not at home, bringing a bottle of chilled wine which she would turn down, just as he planned, sophisticated in the corduroy sport coat he always imagined himself in, scouring the countryside like an avenging angel seeking out old acquaintances and saying, "Look at me. I went away to war and not only didn't die but came back perfect."

He opened the second bottle of wine, pouring it over the rounded pink cubes in his glass, and began dressing. The first bottle of chablis had warmed him, and he felt toward the world as one does shortly after an orgasm, relaxed and kindly. He dressed slowly and lit a cigarette, capping the bottle and putting two packs of matches into his coat pocket.

He stepped into the rain and looked beyond the glow of the yellow bulb above his head and listened as each drop struck distinctly the tin awning. Small rivers had formed in the drowned grass. He did not hurry to his car, worried about his hair as he might have years ago, setting out for Celeste's house.

He carried the glass with him and the wine filled with rain. The interior of the Buick was dry, it muffled the sounds outside, and he leaned on the massive steering wheel and finished the glass and set it on the floor of the backseat.

He had owned a 1953 Plymouth in those days. The engine blew up in Nebraska on a visit to his parents before his induction. He wrote Celeste one letter from basic and was not at all surprised when she didn't reply. Mathews wrote and said she was extraordinarily popular at Boulder, and he had no illusions about what that meant.

The rain parted for the Buick, the reflected streetlights gliding across the bulbous fenders, and he followed a road he could have driven blind.

On this night, two years ago, he was in his third month of basic training. Men were on the moon. Each day was now measured against a moment in the past. Down this darkened street, two years and four months ago, he had driven, she against the passenger door, far and hard against it, he silent, fragile with the feeling, the knowledge, that it was all over. They had finished their last fight. Nothing he did seemed to please her, but that was true of almost everybody he had ever known.

A single blinding streetlight shone at the corner. In the middle of the block, beneath heavy trees, her house was dark.

He came down the street in the same direction he had come that night, watched the parked cars rolling slowly past, and looked at her approaching house. The windows were black. That night, one single yellow window had been lit, the hallway, her parents waiting asleep. She got out of the car before he even put it in Park. Now the rain stopped because the entire street was protected by a tunnel of leaves, and he looked at her house, and the white light at the end of the block shone through the wet tracks left by the rain on his windshield.

He did not know if she, her parents, still lived there. The house silent, each house on the block was dead to life. He pulled at his chablis. He had brought a small sampler whiskey bottle filled with beer to this house one night, opened it in secret with her and she was disgusted and turned her head away.

He eased the automatic shift into D so that the Buick would take him away, because he did not think he could ever take himself away from anything on his own power. At the end of the block he stopped and looked both ways. He had no reason to touch the steering wheel or the gas pedal.

He drank at the wine and looked at the rectangle of black, his rear-view mirror. He dropped the shift into Reverse. The transmission housing at his feet screamed briefly and went silent.

Gorge rising, he delicately lifted the shift into Drive and felt the transmission catch, the car gently rolling forward.

All the way back to the apartment his breath was shallow. He did not touch the wine. He drove darkened side streets and watched for cops. He touched the brakes and gas as little as possible and prayed that his Dynaflow would come through this one last time.

Rolling to the curb and braking, he took a quick swallow of wine, then eased the shift into R.

He would be buying the car from his brother. No Reverse.

CHAPTER 2

The Veterans Administration was on the grounds of the Federal Center in the low rolling hills west along Sixth Avenue. He knew the perimeter fence along Kipling. On his first day as assistant furniture-deliverer, almost penniless, he had passed this place with the driver, an alcoholic in his fifties whose wife managed a run-down green stucco motel on East Colfax. The driver had pulled off the road and prepared to eat his sack lunch. Palmer was bewildered, had expected to return to the shop and hurry back to the dump for a quick lunch. Embarrassed, he told the driver he had planned to buy his lunch, and they went on to a shopping center where Palmer purchased a candy bar. Returning to the truck, he told the driver he had grabbed some chow at a nearby cafe. He was learning the idiom of the working class.

The VA was in a warehouse building designated by a number. He felt at home. He waited his turn in a partitioned room. It was not unlike the employment agency. The pinpoint on his leg itched, some sort of rash like the many rashes which had developed, flared, died and been forgotten during the war. Heat rash, ever present, like mosquitoes. Scratching had become an unconscious act over there. Go to bed angry. The ears never sleep. Scratch your rash and pull another cold soda from the cooler in the MP station.

He tried not to look at the people in the room. Women with husbands. He was glad he was single. He could not bring a wife to such a place. A majority of the clerks were in wheelchairs. When his name was called he took a seat by a gray desk where a clerk, eyeglasses thick, pored over a folder.

A pinpoint on his leg, it had appeared after he was discharged from the army at Ft. Lewis, but he recognized it. In the dump it had begun to spread to his calves and chest, and he scratched it absentmindedly. It would go away. They all did. He was amused when Mike cracked and told him to for Chrissake go see a doctor, the scratching was driving him insane.

"It's not on your records," the vet rep said.

His father had once told him about cuss boxes. In the Solomon Islands, awaiting their discharges from WWII, GIs attempted to stem their foul language by depositing coins in a box each time they slipped up. Palmer had been unaware of the intensity of his scratching.

"It started about a month after I got out of Vietnam. I thought it would go away, but it's spreading."

Wise nodding. "You might have picked it up after you got home. There has to be something about it in your records."

A ripple of guilt. But he was not perpetrating a medical fraud. He was just tired of scratching.

"I didn't get jungle rot in Colorado."

"Did any of your buddies know about the rash?"

"What do you mean?"

"If you can get three or four sworn statements from men who were in your unit asserting you had the rash, the appeals board might qualify you for VA treatment."

The truck driver had taken him to the green stucco motel on the first day he was to be paid. He was broke. Not penny one. They made a delivery on Monaco Parkway and the driver suggested they grab lunch at his place. Palmer was starved, had not eaten breakfast, there is a God. His wife wore a green velvet bathrobe, her hair in curlers. The apartment was ruled by dogs. She disappeared into the kitchen and he turned down a beer, hoping to impress the truck driver with his dedication and conscientiousness. He was only eighteen. She returned and handed him a plate and on it was a sandwich, two slices of brown bread containing what could have been dogfood. He ate it.

Four sworn statements. Both of the man's legs were missing. Palmer scratched at the skin of his breastbone, his fingers slipping beneath his shirt. He was still in the army. He was so happy, if there was a God, he would thank Him that he had not been blinded in the war, had not lost arms or legs or suffered any wounds which would have forced him to depend on the VA for money, for comfort, for dignity. Steaming tropical Pike's Peak.

The rash on his legs burned so he drove home with one hand and scratched with the other. He had entertained the idea that the vet rep would nod understandingly, "I'll see what I can do for you. It's not on your records, but I'm sure the man upstairs will listen to reason." The man pored over the folder, shaking his head. This is a problem.

Palmer walked out.

He had come out one afternoon when he owned the 1953 Plymouth and climbed in and turned the key and met a frightful silence. He opened the hood, perhaps the battery was dry, but no, the battery was gone. A brand-new battery. He was sure the mechanics who had installed it had come in the night, they knew the address, only they knew he had purchased a battery, he had told no one else, and his outrage was now matched, and it was directed at his own stupidity for seeking help from the VA.

There was nowhere else to go, the highway straight, cutting through the center of Denver and across the plains to Kansas. He felt like flooring it and going until he had left this place far behind.

Around seven that evening he went to a bar and had a few beers, then got Mathews on the phone to come to the bar, to bring the evening to a golden finish. But instead Mathews invited him to a party. Palmer agreed to go, Mathews would pick him up. But after he got back to his bar stool, he regretted having accepted the invitation. There would be strangers, the bar stool was soft.

Mathews arrived and they each had a draught, and Palmer told him about the Buick. No reverse and now he owned it. Mathews laughed hard. Outside, Palmer debated whether to follow Mathews in the Buick, because he might want to split early, but Mathews insisted they go together, to talk on the way. They could leave the party whenever Palmer wanted. Palmer was feeling good now, the memory of the VA had softened. He told Mathews about the vet rep, but as he told it, his resentment came back and he found himself fumbling to express his outrage. Mathews only laughed, and said Palmer should go see a private doctor, and put Vietnam behind him.

Palmer's breath came short and he wanted to be back at the bar. After they arrived, Palmer followed Mathews toward a glowing doorway and the sound of music, and hoped he would know someone there. He moved through the living room before Mathews could introduce him around and went into the kitchen where there was beer, feeling self-conscious about his short hair. It might be too short. There was a keg on the back porch but there was a line of people, too. He opened a can from the icebox. The house was filled with women he would never know. He felt transparent, felt there was a way he ought to act. A man took a bite out of a broad-leafed plant and everyone laughed.

He remembered a party in Seattle where he had played poker with the hostess and her dark-eyed solemn friends, who seemed to resent his presence, especially when she helped him because he did not know the order of poker hands. A man rolled joints in pink papers and Palmer managed, because he had not drunk enough, to stop himself from remarking it was ironic how a week earlier he would have been required to bust the man for possession. One player had been in the Infantry in Germany, and when he learned Palmer had been a Military Policeman, he smiled and said, "I hated the fucking MPs."

At midnight Mathews told him to come outside and toss firecrackers, but Palmer stayed at the dining room table, attempting to talk to a woman who might have been sitting on the other side of a brick wall. He was afraid they all knew he had been to Vietnam. They would ask if he killed babies. Firecrackers in the street popped and he looked up, certain someone was watching to see if The Veteran was startled at the noise. He stepped out onto the porch and watched yellow explosions and sparks on the asphalt, the Black Cat belts unbraided or tossed whole.

He did not know anyone. He drank from handed random bottles, then feared he would begin talking about the war, the very last thing he wanted to do.

He looked at each woman closely. He would slice his own or her vocal chords and they would talk only within the limited range of touching, fucking, and clumsiness would never be manifest in the wrong word, and in bed he did not think such a thing existed as the wrong touch.

He emptied his beer and went for another, and the strangers in the kitchen seemed like giants. He took his beer out into the darkness and drank at it and looked at his watch. If it were not so far he would walk home. He should not have made himself dependent on Mathews.

He passed through the house quickly, stumbling, and looked for Mathews but could not find him. He listened to a tune he had never heard before on the stereo, then went back out into the dark and closed his eyes. The car was still there.

He looked at the white lights of downtown Denver and listened for Mathews's discernable laughter. He set his beer down, but it tipped and foamed in the grass. He drank the remainder quickly. Mathews would be in a bedroom probably, sliding his hand into a woman. The grass was damp beneath him and his skin began to itch. He lifted the can but there was no more beer.

A cigarette, two packs of matches, he lit up and looked at the lighted window. That unfamiliar tune was playing again. He wanted more beer but did not want to go inside. Three people came laughing out onto the porch and he sat motionless, anticipating their demand for an explanation of his aloofness, and hating it, and when they went back in without seeing him he did not feel any relief.

The ember of his cigarette touched the foam in the grass and went out. He tossed it into the street near the shredded remains of firecrackers. He drank and smoked on the first night he went to see Celeste, and bought a bottle of Scope, the green mouth deodorant, and washed his mouth into her gutter and threw his cigarettes away so she would not know he smoked. She was multi-virginal. She had never tasted alcohol.

He moved further back into the bushes and tried to count the number of beers he had drunk, but the ground was damp and he stood up afraid someone had been pissing there. He listened for Mathews's voice—it always got louder as Mathews got drunker. He went down to the dark car to see if Mathews might be there, passed out or fucking. The doors were locked. He longed to climb inside. He did not know where he wanted to be, but he did not want to be here.

He felt no progress, remembered how he had refused to go to parties in high school. Poster parties, girls in tight shorts, revealing what was hidden under the drab and sexless brown Catholic uniform dresses which officially were meant to lift a financial burden from the backs of parents sending their children to the parochial schools but which everyone knew was the last desperate denial of the vagina. He had refused to go to the dances, Pep Club, Homecoming, Prom. He was a social functional-illiterate.

He went through the house again and did not see Mathews, and his sense of freedom spiraled to earth. Standing outside by the car, he felt chained to the ground by his balls, and nothing to do about it because Mathews had disappeared. Nothing to hit. Impotent at the desk of an entity. "There's nothing I can do for you. It's not on your records."

It did not take as long as he had imagined to walk to the bar where he had left his car. His anger increased as he grew sober, and he looked forward to downing a few fresh beers before getting into his car which could take him quickly wherever he might wish to go with no backing up.

His car was not there when he arrived, and his hands began to shake violently at his sides. He walked the block around but it was gone. He touched the keys in his pants. As he walked home he thought of the things he would do to the persons who had stolen it, should he encounter them. Pound a forehead to the pavement. Bludgeon with a tire-iron. They would be teenagers. Break all the fingers of each hand, leaving them still alive in the street to be found later by the police, not hurt bad enough to press charges, but hurt bad enough that they would never forget it.

When he got home the car was in front of his apartment. His astonishment turned to anger and he entered and woke up Mike demanding to know what the car was doing there. Someone in the bar had seen Palmer leave with Mathews. His brother had dropped by later with a friend and took the car home, assuming Palmer wouldn't want to leave it parked on the street all night. Just doing him a favor.

When they were children, Mike had taken Palmer's Christmas bike to Lakeside Amusement Park where it was stolen. It was not the loss of the bike but the knowledge that he could never be certain any of his possessions would be there when he wanted them which had outraged him. He had made no progress at all.

He left the apartment and climbed into the car. There was no place to go, but he drove it around the block so the car would again be his. He understood now a saying, the meaning of which had eluded him when he first heard it as a child: the road to Hell is paved with good intentions.

CHAPTER 3

He had lifted weights at one time in the war, and the resistance of the bar rising in front of his face was sufficient reason alone for the activity. When the bar was removed, his arms ached for the return of the pressure, but when he gave up lifting weights and became weaker, his arms eventually ceased to anticipate, to look forward to, that pressure.

He told Mike he would be looking for a new place. He wanted to apologize for his anger on the night the car had disappeared, but he was not sure his brother knew how angry he really had been, and so he said nothing. He had not seen Mathews in three weeks and no longer wanted to see him or anyone he had known before he went to war.

Palmer had over two thousand dollars in separation money and was receiving unemployment, but he began thinking about going to college, an idea which at first repelled and even angered him when Mike brought it up one afternoon as they watched the Broncos fulfill their destiny as eternal losers. His brother's intentions were innocent, it seemed to him a fine way to get free money, but his brother wasn't aware of Palmer's hatred of unasked-for advice, and his hatred of school in general. Two roads to Hell. He refused comment. They watched the football team suffer total devastation.

A week later, Palmer drove past the UCD building downtown and remembered that his brother had taken night classes there a few years ago, just after they moved into the dump, and the possibility of going back to school entered his mind unopposed because, as his brother said, it seemed like a fine way to get free money.

But it was school, and the concept of college was overwhelming, a complex endeavor with which he did not wish to burden his life. In six months he would be out looking for a job, but the GI Bill promised to feed him for four years. As a child he had been a quitter, timid of steering his own destiny, the reason he had ended up in Vietnam instead of the Playboy Mansion, and so one afternoon he picked up an application from the admissions office and visited the school vet rep in a burst of sheer will. The idea of sitting at a desk and letting a teacher tell him anything about life revolted him, but the idea of getting a job was almost debilitating.

He sent the application in quickly, and that same day he received three offers to renew his GI insurance before it was too late. He wadded each unopened envelope and threw them hard against the wall, and as each ball of crackling paper hit the floor he felt good.

He was advised he must take the ACT test. He took it a few weeks later at his old high school, and it seemed to him he was going through some kind of appalling regression. He had begun to grow a beard. He looked like a bum and was embarrassed to be sitting in a room with kids, teenagers, who were going on to college for, perhaps, all the wrong reasons. He was embarrassed because he felt grown up, shaggy and sophisticated among children he felt inferior to in ways he could not define, and in ways he could; none of them looked like bums, and some were bigger than he.

He felt no antipathy toward the students, but the icy wall he had always felt as a teenager between himself and adults, teachers, priests, all authorities, emerged briefly when the high school counselor, in innocence, told him he was fortunate he had been squeezed into this testing session because the next one was not until spring. He succeeded in not grinning and nodding, the response instilled in him throughout life which covered the emotion summed up in such phrases as: Why don't you drop dead, asshole.

He heard nothing from UCD and did not care because already he had come up with newer plans. It occurred to him one morning as he peered briefly out the window at the very thinnest whitewash of snow on the ground that he hated snow and winter and that he ought to move to California before his money ran out. It was the first snow of winter and melted before noon, and it held a promise of dead batteries, frozen engine blocks, burst radiators, and icy slides through intersections, and fender-benders and far worse. Colorado was not justified. There was no reason mankind had to take this abuse from nature. The gold, the silver, the mountains had been sucked dry.

Mike told him it was not likely the Buick would survive a trip across the Rockies to California anyway, and that it was dangerous and irresponsible to even think of driving that far without reverse. Palmer told him that was the only way to go. The remark irritated his brother in a way which surprised Palmer. He realized Mike had taken the idea seriously, so he agreed it was an impractical idea, and said he had no intention of doing anything so dumb, an expression he felt his brother needed to hear.

He thought often of taking up weight lifting, but the basement apartment had such a low ceiling that it would be difficult. There was a public gym in a park half a mile away, but it was too much trouble to go there. He missed the good feel, the pressure of the bar of steel, and told himself that once he found a new apartment, he would lift weights again as he had done briefly during the war when he had so badly needed a tangible resistance.

CHAPTER 4

Celeste is engaged.

The veneer of porcelain which covered each object in his kitchen was blue in the light of the small TV balanced on the cold burners of the stove.

Engaged and possibly a baby on the way, Brie had said. His chair tilted back cramped against the beer-stained wall, his brother asleep and sick with a cold in the other room, Palmer peeled away page after page of the Sunday paper stolen on Saturday night, and glanced at want ads, nibbling the possibilities of work he did not really need.

Buried in the untouched layer of dust beneath his bed which had not been moved since the day he left for Vietnam, he had found, while doing nothing more than marveling at this furry matted unchanged thing, a small elongated prong of metal used by paper carriers to open Denver Post boxes, a key his brother had not given back after his brief stint at a paper station supervising young Chicano entrepreneurs near the projects on Santa Fe Drive a few years back, boys who could fire rubber bands with deadly accuracy.

How could Celeste be engaged?

Time was supposed to have come to a standstill when he went away. Time had cuckolded him.

The pages of the newspaper came away like the skins of an onion, his fingers black with newsprint, the wetness around the red rims of his eyes might be blamed on wine. He was secure, having gone on unemployment—a veteran of the war gets sixty-eight bucks a week. Want ads are like blackjack.

Turn that next card over. Life's a gamble, once said a friend who drove a cab at night. It's a gamble. Men get killed driving cabs. Cops get killed. You hate the tension until it goes away, and then everything is cottage cheese and milk of magnesia.

Brie, you woman, the only girl in high school who smoked cigarettes with impunity, she had stroked the stubble beneath his chin in English class one day (she said "God I love the way that feels") when he had not shaved because it made him feel like a rebel and he'll never ever change. She was light-years ahead of her time. Her hair was white. She dated College Men and each afternoon a dark stranger cruised into the parking lot in a blue 1949 Chevy and she climbed in and disappeared and nobody objected to this stranger in their midst, in their Senior Parking Lot, because he belonged to Brie who is married now and working in a Near-New Shoppe because she, at age twenty-four (held back two grades by the nuns, she was an older woman, God, no wonder he got along so well with her back then, she kissed him lightly on the lips in the school parking lot at noon after he had loaned her his Zippo to light a smoke) is now a Bored Housewife.

The wetness around his eyes is for Brie.

He looked up the TV movies for the coming week and skimmed the Sunday comics which no longer made him smile. Letters to the editor. Each poor writer suffering from a messiah complex. "Dear Editor . . ." He composed letters in his mind which he would never send.

Still half a bottle of wine left, now Vin Rose, stronger than pink chablis. Morning libation. Too late for drive-ins. The Lakeshore. The dangerous Lakeshore Drive-In where high school kids go in groups, sometimes sneaking in by hiding in trunks, because the Lakeshore is legendary for its danger. Gangs of ethnics rule that theatre by night. Oh yes, it's true. Chicanos. One night three kids from North High were knifed. Oh yes, it's true.

So we all went in one car and drank beer and smoked cigars, and went to the pisser (the restroom, but only candy-asses say restroom) in groups. The Lakeshore was basic training. You learned to sneer. Never any celluloid tits. Not like today. Back then, go see a movie about teenage girls on a slave farm, no tits. Shit.

Would Brie have gone with them to the drive-in back in those days? She had tits.

Now she works in the Near-New Shoppe, and still smokes, and recognized my eyes above my beard, she knew who I was.

There were no good used books in the Near-New Shoppe, only a lot of romances. Brie was standing behind the counter, chewing gum. She knew all about Celeste. Astronomical pattern of friendships. Brie once dated a CU man, and had met Celeste one night, it was complex, but how many times had he met strangers who knew kids he had gone to grade school with twelve years ago? Celeste is engaged to some guy. Brie went to a party with friends and ran into her. Yeah, engaged over a year ago. Yeah. Yeah. "Why don't you go see her, Palmer?"

The Mini-Art Theatre. Triple sizzling XXX. Adults only. Welton Street. He looked down the porno columns. Where is the legendary Victory Theatre? Did the city tear that down, too? Where is thy ad? Ortega went there every week. Ortega had stories to tell. He owned a trunk full of smut he had purchased in a shop next door. Where is that little Puerto Rican truck driver? Where is everybody?

OPEN 24 HOURS.

Brazen, emboldened, the empire which never sleeps. Palmer sat forward on the kitchen chair and squinted at the ad. He looked at his watch. The bars were now closed, but this place was OPEN 24 HOURS.

His mind began to race.

Like a boat it moved, swayed around corners. This would have been the perfect drive-in car. 1954 Buick Special, a truly mythical backseat.

He should not have let Celeste get away. No guts.

He lifted the half bottle of red wine and drank at it with impunity. A cold beer in each pocket. He had never been inside a Denver X-rated theatre. He was crazy. He would be assaulted in the cheap seats.

He drank at the wine and guided the car (you don't *drive* a Buick) down Federal onto Speer Boulevard. It was magic, there were no cops out tonight, the streets were empty, he was alone in an abandoned city.

Engaged and possibly a kid on the way, prima facie evidence that someone had finally put it to her. Nailed her. Banged her. Fucked her eyeballs out. What a terrible thing to think about a woman about to be married in a church.

He did not know downtown. It was a city of alleys and no-parking zones for furniture deliverers. (He once spent three hours picking lint off blue chairs in a lawyer's office.) Where was Luby's Chevrolet, the summer work of high school friends? Leveled. But LaFite's was still there, big and white with an alley where he and Mathews once passed two bums scrounging wet lettuce in a dumpster. One leaned, arms akimbo, into the car window. "Listen boys, I'm not gonna bullshit ya." Gravel voice. "I'm trying to get money together for a bottle of wine." They gave him nickels from their teenage pockets. They found a penny baked in the rear window and gave it to him. Palmer had never before seen men eating garbage.

The Mini-Art Theatre, tiny yellow marquee bulbs racing, red tinsel, it glowed in the middle of the dark street, a painted woman.

He drove past and looked. And did he not once say to Mathews in Catholic youth macho, "I'd like to toss a stick of dynamite into the lobby of the Victory Theatre" and save the world. Little Catholics doing good deeds for the Pope.

A week of prayer and meditation, a Retreat. He read a science-fiction novel instead of religious pamphlets. The nun caught him. Dale Simpson claimed he once snuck into the Victory Theatre, and Palmer got a boner just thinking about it.

He drove around the block. Twenty-four hours. It seemed odd that dirty theatres existed, people fucking on the screen. When you're a kid you grab looks in men's magazines in the grocery, the unthinkable hope is to see a woman completely naked, but you never really believe you will, not even your wife, vague woman.

Ten years old, smoking cigarettes under a lilac bush in the backyard. "Don't you know what a whore is?" Visions of a straggly-haired woman. "You give her a dollar and she'll let you do anything to her for one hour." A few moments of thoughtful consideration. "Gosh—I'd fuck her."

The cashier's booth was draped in heavy purple velvet, he could not see the man's face, the soul of the perverted heart universally understood. No one would be seeing his beers, one in each pocket of his coat. He passed through velvet curtains, he could see no faces. On the screen, in technicolor, a woman's lips slid up and down a colossal cock.

There might have been ten people in the theatre, ten heads above ten seats at any rate. God knows what might be taking place below those tombstone rows. He walked slowly down a side aisle, far away from anyone. Would there be queers? The projector clicked, whirred high above and behind him, accompanied by giant sucking sounds. Safe in an unbroken seat, he punched a beer quietly open in the folds of his coat pocket and surreptitiously sipped.

Bigger than life the movies are. The screen might have been called small a decade earlier, but it was larger than the burgeoning mini-twins new throughout the city. Two men pumping away on a sprawled woman. Each feature lasted barely an hour, but he wouldn't leave when it got boring because it was like turning the pages of a dirty magazine. The next picture might be even better.

The first movie ended and he gazed at the gum-streaked back of the seat in front of him wondering if brilliant lights would rise, exposing a theatre as bleak and empty as his soul.

It had not been difficult laying with the small-breasted hairless women of Vietnam, rain pelting window screens, accented laughter. Ten bucks. They believed everything you said and indicated it with a nodding of the head. They smelled bad and yet the odor was friendly. Mouths. Cunts. It was a juvenile paradise.

A poorly drawn, crude in many senses, cartoon—simple black-and-white animation of an ape with an enormous penis sodomizing everyone he encountered.

The acting was pitiful, lifelike. A woman pretending to be her own twin seducing her husband to learn whether he would remain faithful. An orgy, cocks and cunts in a badly lighted motel room, sperm launched. Actors gazed blankly at the camera, and in that moment became real. Limp dicks plopped out of pussies and were reinserted.

An overlong, ten-minute blowjob. Fire-engine red lips and yellow teeth, blue veins. The celluloid wad hit her face, dripped from her nose, tongue swiping it between her lips.

He turned cautiously, did not wish to give anyone the idea he was lonesome, but heard sounds at the back of the theatre. Two policemen stood watching. A raid, certainly. A Regis High School friend said that he once left a porno theatre not ten minutes before it was raided. But these police only watched, and after a while Palmer turned and they were gone.

The women on the screen would not smile, would not grin and laugh the way fucking women do. Somber, the men beneath them thrusting, somber as though not a part of this thing. Even the women in Vietnam had laughed. Oh those Vietnam whores. They had taken him so far away from the suburbs he didn't think he would ever get back. Brie, did something happen to you, too? What happened to all of us?

A naked woman with her back against a door, listening to moaning couples beyond. She is masturbating, fingers twisting her glistening hairy lips. Her skin like dark wood, she has freckles, green eyes, and her fingers disappear. Palmer opens the last beer while two people enter her room and fuck and suck.

You were only a kid. All eighteen-year-olds are hopeless. Celeste was wrapped in plastic, is gone forever, it doesn't matter. In Vietnam you gave Suzy a toy Christmas flute and she rode past the compound for weeks blowing it, and everyone kept laughing, and you awoke in the night with a grin because you always knew when Suzy was riding by with her pimp.

The assistant gives the dentist a blowjob. A black woman sits on the executive's face. The captain and the sailor both enter the blonde, never saw two men do it to a woman at once. Interesting. A rainbow fluttering on a white wall, technicolor shadows, it's only pictures of things that happened when you blinked.

The first film began again, grainy and dim in a crimson room, no dialogue. In the army he had once gone to a San Francisco skin-flick. The movie was black-and-white, the woman took an hour undressing, and the leering psychiatrist only bobbled her tits. No fucking. No cunt hair cocks passion. Xylophone music dubbed. He didn't know his way around the city. All the real skin was on Columbus Avenue. He walked down Market Street and was lured into a jewelry store by a pushy salesman who knew him by the shine of his shoes. He and a buddy once went down into the city and two beautiful women in a blue Mustang cruised by their bus stop. They looked like fashion-magazine models. Blonde and brunette. The brunette was driving. "Want a date?" the blonde said in a voice softer than perfume. She was smiling like a centerfold. The smile looked so damn sincere and probably even was. She was searching for money, but who wasn't? The world was filled with beautiful women, but Palmer and his buddy only had three bucks between them. "No thanks," they said, grinning like idiots.

He set the empty beer on the floor with its twin. The mystery had fled the theatre. He had to piss. Part of his apprehension was the possibility of being caught with beer. Thrown out of a porno theatre for drinking, how low can a man sink?

The restroom was in the basement, in the rear. Standing, he was drunker than he thought and he wanted more wine. A man entered and Palmer forced himself to piss. When the man left, Palmer looked at machines on the wall. Rainbow-colored contraceptives. He put in a quarter and bought a membership in the Transcontinental Sex Club. Busty broad, dark-nippled maja grinning. Sign your name here. Good for one free fuck. Void where prohibited ha ha.

CHAPTER 5

On the morning of the first deep snow of winter, he awoke from a dream of death, his limbs frozen, his hair erect, his stomach a nest of plastic snakes. He lay like a child awakened from a nightmare. He had dreamed of a blackened carcass hanging upside down, slit at the neck, the body disgorging itself in polished chunks of a dark sludge, and he backed so far away from it he came out of sleep.

His eyelashes were moist, his throat dry. He went to the kitchen for a glass of water, brought it to his bed and sat sipping and waiting for the mood of the dream to leave him.

Mike was at work. It was noon and Palmer was exhausted with eleven hours' sleep. He held the curtain up and looked out at the snow, six inches and still falling. He had not seen snow in two years. He tried to work up some nostalgia, but in fact he despised it. The Buick probably wouldn't start.

He had drunk one bottle of wine last night and fell asleep immediately because he had been drunk each night for the past two weeks and his nervous system had finally abandoned him.

Yesterday his mind awoke, but his body would not respond. Each finger leaden, he could not move his eyelids, and he was glad.

He arose now and twisted the valve on the small brown tin gas heater on the floor against the wall and held his palms above the hot surface. His forearms and fingers had an aching weakness which he felt could only be alleviated by lifting barbells.

He put a pan of water on to boil and got dressed. Gloves and a knit hat for a short journey, he stepped into the wall of cold and hopped through the snow to the mailbox.

Breakfast was a box of Kraft Dinner and a Coke. It had been weeks since he had eaten like a human being. He entertained the notion of going each day to a restaurant and having a square meal, not unlike an army meal, but . . .

Another 68-dollar check from the State. They were piling up. He would not be touching the cash from these checks until The Thaw.

A letter from UCD. You have been accepted. Those D minuses in high school Latin were paying off.

His friends used to talk about buying a few acres in the Rockies to escape Modern Life, a perennial plan. They would never do it and he would never go back to school. He gazed at the silken folds of his melted cheese and macaroni. Almost three hundred bucks a month for four years. A little memento of the war.

He finished his meal and searched the channels for a TV show, turned the sound off on a baseball game and watched muted fouls. The walls of the apartment, plastered concrete, were cold, and he turned the heat up. He would not be driving across the Continental Divide in this weather. Either California would wait until spring, or he would take a bus. No more flying. Anyway, the Buick wouldn't make it, even in nice weather. Although if it broke down on the road in a spot chosen by the death angel of vintage heaps it would not be such a calamity. This was America, not a lonely road in Vietnam. The car breaks down, you walk. Shoe leather wears out, you thumb.

Without sound, the TV commercials revealed themselves: desperate, startling graphics and facts impotent without trumpets. A woman holding a can of deodorant, lips moving, an actress who will say anything for money.

The room grew too hot, he was drowsy. He lowered the heat and turned up the TV, switched to a Dead End Kids dubbed in Spanish, then turned it off.

His body felt like a giant knuckle which begged to be popped. He looked at his splayed palms. Pot fascination. He had first gotten stoned in the war, and had stared at his arms and fingers and realized he was a system of bicycle hand-brake cables. Stared for hours flexing his fingers trying to catch his brain giving the command, but it was like trying to see your own eyes move in a mirror.

He listened to the hiss of gas. How could the government allow gas pipes to run throughout a city? The bodies of gas victims are said to be black, bloated. He'd never seen a dead man, not even in war. The soldier who blew his own head off was taken away beneath a poncho liner. Doughboys stepped through the rotted corpses of trench dead, their boots sinking through ribcage like ash. Gas masks had more than one function.

He had dreamed of knife blades slicing his belly, dreamed of cats, vicious spitting cats clinging to his body, claws digging in painlessly as he imagined a starfish might grip. How he hated those dreams.

The money would run out after six months. He did not know what he was supposed to do. Grade school. High school. College or the army. Then you get a job based on the skills acquired over the preceding fifteen years. He had expected to die in Vietnam. He had made no plans.

He turned the record player on, it was a toy, and he put on the 45 record he had found at a furniture store on Santa Fe Drive which had a strange little department dealing in golden oldies. It was the melody which had played again and again at the party where he had parted company with Mathews, a record he might never have found, believing it to be one of those melodies you hear only once and lose forever, had he once caught the end of it on a distant static Oklahoma station while returning one night from a bar. "In the Mood" by Glenn Miller. On the flip side was "String of Pearls." The music with which his parents had danced off to war.

He played it every day and thought of Jimmy Stewart. A woman in a bar on Pearl Street had insisted the role of Glenn Miller had been portrayed by Steve Allen. His brother Mike had asked why he wallowed in that old crap, and Palmer said Big Band would outlive all other forms of twentieth-century music. It was the soundtrack of every film he had, as a child, seen on TV. Black-and-white messages. At the age of ten he was stunned to learn that all the Little Rascals were grown up, the girls had children. He had entertained the fantasy that he could go to Hollywood and talk to Alfalfa.

If the 45 wore out, he would return to the furniture store and buy a new one. He wondered what had become of the thick 33 rpm records which had belonged to his parents. They shattered so easily.

The snow would melt, it would be warm in a few days, the car would start. Celeste would be home for Christmas break. He had all the time in the world. His final obligation had been to go to a physician and obtain a prescription for a balm which would eradicate the rash. He would be through with Vietnam.

He found his hours becoming like the hours spent in guard towers in Vietnam. Reviewing your past life, as people who have purportedly gone beyond the pale, only to return to tell the non-believers. Every sin, every flaw exposed. And some say that's what hell is all about.

He played the record one more time, then forced himself to turn the machine off as he had forced himself to put the Buick into gear. He did not believe he would ever tire of this song. Glenn Miller had died in WWII in a plane crash in the English Channel. Palmer saw the man in a white tuxedo going down in a bomber, and every musical note was that artist trying to say something which he had never quite been able to put into words.

His fear of flying kept Palmer from taking an R&R to Australia or the sex pits of Bangkok or to Hawaii or Hong Kong, his fear of flying exceeding even his fear of the war itself. "We all have to die sometime," his buddies had said. "I didn't say I was afraid of dying, I said I was afraid of flying." Futility.

Someday he would listen to his parents' record collection, play each melody once, and find out who that silent man was who went off to WWII. Returned. Married. Kids. Thirty years with the same company. Six-foot-two, and came home from the Solomon Islands weighing one-twenty. There was a diary, two handwritten books among the souvenirs of war in the canvas bag dusty in the basement of their Wichita home. What became of it all? A grass hula skirt. A blue glass cowboy-boot bottle. Stacks of letters to Palmer's mother-to-be and an album of photographs. Palmer had his own canvas bag now, had packed his army equipment away, hidden his uniforms in the back of the closet, had thrown out his MP notebook from Ft. Gordon.

He went to the closet and carefully removed his green Class A uniform and laid it on the bed. Three medals. There should have been another, but he never got around to purchasing the fourth at a PX. All he had was the written orders, they never gave him the medal itself. A lot of things aren't like the movies.

He put his uniform away carefully. The thing would rot at the creases and disintegrate someday, now that it was a part of history, something to show the children he would never beget.

He returned to the record player and put Glenn Miller on, just once more, the music which transcends time and knows no audience.

The snow would melt, it would be warm in a few days. He applied the ointment to the red and itching patches which had spread from his legs to his arms and chest. He didn't think he would be going to college after all.

CHAPTER 6

It had begun with the cautious eager exploration of a virgin examining for the first time a body unlike his own and then it became a weekly adventure, getting comfortable with the theatre, and then it became something he did because he did not know what else to do, and so he quit going there.

At a bar in Glendale he met a woman and bought her four drinks and could think of nothing to say because he did not have talking in mind. He wanted to tell her about the skin-flicks, and wanted to tell her about the whores of Vietnam, as if this talk might disarm her and let her see the nothing-to-be-ashamed-of side of the lust he was afraid she would end up denying him.

They parted in the bar, and a week later met again, and sober he felt antipathy toward her, although she was a beautiful woman. It was the same barrier he had encountered with the woman in San Francisco, present and unassailable. It had the earmarks of impotence, but it was not physical. He could not maintain a conversation without the fear that at any moment he might begin talking at the top of his voice.

Mathews once said he had never "paid for it" and never would. "Don't knock it until you've tried it," Palmer said, and as the words left his mouth he felt somewhat like an asshole.

In the parking lot he attempted to neck with the woman, whose black, shark-like eyes accused him while refusing to reveal what was "really" going through her mind, if anything. Lips dry, kisses dishonest, he felt he ought to be someplace else, doing something with a purpose. Awkward caressing of thighs, a lifeless hand on her pussy, it was something like impotence, and he found himself in the awful position of trying to make light of it. Laughing couples emerged from the bar, speeding off into their own nights. He wanted very badly to be away from her. It was too easy. It was too difficult. He took her in for another drink and went home.

You go to the gate and ask the MP on duty if he will let you bring a whore onto the compound. You have a ready reserve of anger, knowing that the MP holds life-and-death sway over your satisfactions. You are a little bit drunk and you hope you know the guard, and when he says yes you step outside the fence and flag down a pimp on a Honda and there is a brief exchange. He drives off and you wait in the shadows hoping she will at least be pretty, and at any moment a CID man or some officer might come by and you're going to get an Article 15 and lose a stripe, then she hops off the rear of her pimp's Honda and you take her tiny hand and hurry along the barracks and into your cubicle, and you know she has the clap but you don't give a shit anymore because in a minute or so your cock is going to be hammering away.

In the afternoon, he would awaken and the room would be filled with gray light. His brother never seemed to be there anymore. His diet was boiling bags and Coke. He bought an ounce of pot and smoked it in a week, coming down only long enough to take himself to a Safeway. He ate a lot of tuna fish. He watched the small blue buzzing TV for hours without moving, delighting in the fast-paced rhythm of commercials and the tragedy of technical difficulties. It was an effort to rise once a day and take a shit, his only feat. He liked shitting while stoned, it lasted forever.

He thought of going to a porno movie stoned, but paranoia blossomed, the unthinkable problem of getting downtown in his Buick at three a.m. stoned, a cop on every corner. He abandoned the idea, but wished he had understanding friends who would take him there, like a cripple to Lourdes.

His dreams of death were unchanging, a knife blade slitting his intestines accompanied by a foul odor, a glistening straight-razor smell. He awoke from these dreams exhausted. He did not believe in them, but he had no control over them, and his anguish was real. He could take himself away physically from anything but that.

He quit answering the door. He left the phone off the hook. His brother had failed to pay the rent two weeks running and one morning Palmer was awakened by an appalling pounding. He thought the house was on fire. At the door stood a huge man in overalls, thick spectacles, crewcut. He might have been a farmer. He was the nephew of the landlord. "Got any rent!"

Now he ignored all sounds at the door and the occasional voice he might recognize. Mike was disturbed at this because it was incomprehensible to him that anyone could refuse to answer a door or a telephone, as if there was something slightly illegal about it.

Whenever he thought of Celeste, it was with a desire to return to the night four years ago when they had parted, and be the person he is now. It was the desire of a thirteen-year-old to be seven, "and know what I know now about sex." He could not talk to women he did not know. They would need to know his entire past to comprehend what he is saying at this very moment.

On a Friday afternoon, he went for a supply of beer and food and began drinking as soon as he got home, turning the TV dials and listening to Glenn Miller. He read through the evening paper and looked at the titles of the porno movies. Before, he had been drawn, but now he had to force himself to view the animal at work. It was light against a wall.

His brother came home, cleaned up and left. The odor of shower mist and soap faded from the apartment. Brief activity and gone. Well, they did not have much to talk about anymore. Palmer said he would be moving out but hadn't yet. Whenever Mike answered the door, Palmer took a shower.

At two in the morning he was reading the ads for legitimate films. He set the paper aside and opened another beer. He had driven up Lawrence Street and down Larimer the night before, as he and friends had done in high school, looking for the prostitutes they would never buy. He coasted along Colfax. The strip joints were all going bottomless.

He got up and took a six-pack of beer from the refrigerator and left the apartment. The first snow had melted under a hot front which had rolled across the state. It was shirt-sleeve weather, but he took his coat because the pockets might be needed to hide beer. He climbed into his car. His parents had owned a Buick, same year and model, it had been a behemoth in his memories, fire-engine red. It had smelled like his childhood. He had seen its disintegration. It was now a cube of steel in a junkyard.

The Buick might have been designed for a drunk. It did not respond quickly. It moved out slowly and rolled to stops. It lumbered. He felt giddy whenever he got behind the miniature wheel of a Volkswagen. An open can cooled his crotch as he watched for police and laughed remembering the egocentric universe of teenagers who commit underage crimes certain that every badge in the city is looking for juvenile offenders. His friends had cruised dark streets quickly emptying cans of beer, Hurry, here comes a cop! Young Catholics like to get caught. Forgiveness is a fix.

The car rolled up the 23rd Street viaduct, the city sank. Below, the red warning railroad lights of Union Station glittered on the tracks which fanned from the terminal to the river. A train passed, the viaduct bounced, white smoke floated in the cantilever beams.

He did not know Denver. His past was suburban. Denver was the buildings where his parents went when they "went out." Mother in make-up, the unfamiliar laughter of his father with dinner guests. Denver was for grown-ups.

Down the viaduct, an overcoat bum in khaki stood with a shoulder against a wall, a blanket of newspapers flaking and sliding up the gutter. Palmer recognized nothing. High school nights in this part of town, endless railroad streets and maroon brick warehouses in the dark, it had been, and still was, a maze, and he felt good not knowing exactly where he was.

Buick tires hammering steel rails crossing the streets where redbrick emerged from patches in asphalt like a rash, boxcars in the shadows, he pulled at his beer and peered up each cross-street. The odor of coal was in the air.

In San Francisco he had fooled himself on Market Street. Colfax is too bright. He wanted the dark of the Denver Bottoms where the whorehouses once thrived. Mattie Silks. He passed the bars on Larimer Street. When he was twenty he had entered the Ginn Mill before the block was torn down and the bar had been moved nearer the river. A one a.m. dare, it was not enough to drive the old streets tossing Tiparillos and feeling sorry for the derelicts, he had wanted to go in, but his friends wouldn't. He wanted to stand in dark doorway nineteenth-century museum architect alcoves and flick cigarette butts with real bums. He went alone into the Ginn Mill and bought a beer, drank, then spilled it. When the bartender asked for his I.D. he ran out of the bar. Nearly caught, underage. His friends waiting in the car laughed at him, but he did it.

Up Blake, down Wazee, he looked for what he wished would be there, prostitutes walking. The respectable people were locked asleep, the night people were laughing. He drove down Larimer Street and passed an open door. She was black and leaning in the light and her eyes followed him as he passed. It was time to go around the block.

Sweet apprehension, it was the high school girl you barely knew, alone at the bus stop. Drive around the block and pretend you're going to pick her up and drive to the mountains and talk about The Future.

Her shadow lay across the sidewalk, ink, the rectangle doorway light loud with voices and music. She was still there and this time he kept his eyes on hers as he passed, and she did not turn away. When he came around the third time she was not there, but in the lit room there were black men in hats laughing, and there were children. He slowed this time, you have to slow before you stop, and went around the block finishing a can of beer and opening another to have something in his hand.

Headlights on, the engine running, tires soft against the curb, he saw a black man fall laughing out the door. The man strode past the car and stopped to peer in.

Palmer nodded, "That woman . . ."

"What woman? Nice car," the man said.

"That woman in the doorway. Is she . . .?"

"Is she who? Hey man, you got any more beers?"

Palmer tore one from the plastic rings.

"Yeah man, I know what you're talking about. Sure. You got the cash, you got to talk to her husband though."

"Where is he?" Palmer said.

An old man, young in a wide-brimmed hat and an overcoat slung across his shoulders, a cape, a pimp selling his woman, a tacky Denver pimp with dull shoes.

"I can fix you up. This beer is cold. Thanks." The man went back into the room lit with laughter.

Palmer looked down Larimer. This place, a storefront still open in the night, it once must have been an open fruit-and-vegetable market, now boarded up, cinderblock and plywood and painted black and turned into a gathering place between an apartment building three-stories and a Mexican restaurant now closed. A police car passed. He waited for it to back up, what is a white boy doing here, even though 22nd and Larimer is not a black part of town. The police car went away. The woman looked out from the doorway, a paper cup in her hand. The staggering man returned. Twenty dollars.

Palmer wanted her to come with him. To his place, to a better part of town. The fear was like a fresh drink of water and he wanted to go into the room full of laughing people but felt his presence would be resented. No, she could not leave in his car. They would be going upstairs.

"My husband asked why you didn't come in and ask yourself?" leading him up the narrow dusty carpeted stairs. He didn't reply. She held his hand, led him down a vast silent hallway of open doors. In one room, on a bed, lay a Mexican girl with a boy, with another boy sitting alongside on a folding chair. They looked at him. At the end of the hall was a telephone surrounded by ink scrawls. There was a Coke machine. She took him into a clean shabby room and closed the door. The bedspread was pink, a furrowed mattress. He felt the presence of alien people—he did not belong and he felt at home. Celeste was a Methodist and went to church. She wore perfume. She would die with milk on her breath.

The woman sat him on the bed, the money was in her husband's pocket. "You don't hafta take off your shirt," she said. He smiled and didn't even finish taking off his pants. She was sweet.

He had not understood what it was Celeste wanted. A nineteen-year-old boy expected to comprehend the mind of a woman-about-to-become-Woman, he had never even been in the presence of a naked tit. His underwear was already wet and growing cold, his cock bent slightly, irritated with leakage, sore and unfulfilled, the legacy of teenage automobile front-seat encounters. You think it will never come to fruition, will always have to be endured. Celeste kept her distance, pressed against the far door. Now he knows, she was bundling herself against his oafishness while she was vainly searching for the key to melt this chill. If he touched her, the night might crumble like ash. He had made the first crude suggestion he had ever made to a girl in his life, but not the last one. Celeste was a virgin and wore it like a training bra. They could not connect.

The woman was truly sweet. Her eyes were large. He wanted to weep and wished the room was theirs. He stood and pulled his pants on, his mind soft. She waited as he zipped up and walked next to him down the stairs and outside.

"See you," a practiced farewell. He walked to his car and felt the blow. His car was locked, the keys were inside.

The night quickened around him and the laughter from the room surged. His mouth stale, he touched his shirt pocket and saw the cigarettes inside on the seat, the beer in the back. Sobriety began to hurt.

The police car passed again and he waited until it turned before working at the doors and windows. Drunk parking. He wanted to go home. The room was emptying. The staggering man had left his empty beer can on the hood. A window would have to be broken, it was no mystery, but his hands were empty and there was not a thing on this strangely clean street. He dismissed the idea of using an elbow.

He touched the windows, invisible walls, heard a voice and turned to see the pimp with his wife disappearing up the stairs in the dim foyer light. His groin relaxed, numb. He looked into the gutter for something to break the glass.

The police car passed again and he waved. "I locked myself out." A young blond cop, fresh for the morning patrol. The sky had changed tones. The cop handed him an enormous flashlight and Palmer swung at the wing window, though he had been told they are more expensive to replace. He handed the torch back, thanked the cop and reached inside. Shattered glass lay across the front seat like giant crystals of salt. He brushed at them gently. The seat covers were new.

Life is easy. He inserted the key and pressed the gas to silence. He looked at the extended headlight knob.

Squatting at the curb, he gazed at the pale orange life dying inside the molded headlight glass. The battery was dead. He looked at the third story of the apartment building, leaned his forehead, as if to hide his face, against the fender.

There is no punishment, but there is stupidity and conceit. He stood and gazed at the paling sky. Eyes stinging, it was exhaustion, the Inanimate Object the most belittling of opponents. Just a ton of metal now, its heart had stopped.

The beer on the floor was warm. He sat gingerly on the seat, crumbs of glass tumbling. His cheeks were warm. He unbuttoned the top of his shirt and scratched at a patch of jungle rot on his breastbone. There were no gas stations open at this time of the morning. He looked at his wrist, but he had wisely left his watch at home. The sweat and crust of his cock began to itch. His bunkmate in basic training had been morose for weeks after a blowjob in Clarksville. The other GI had fucked her and got the clap and waddled for a week. "How can I face my girl after doing a thing like that?" An inconsolable ploughboy from Nebraska. "At least you didn't get the clap," Palmer suggested. Her husband was probably up there right now, counting her money.

He looked at the third-story window faint in the coming light. The ignition silent between his fingers, he cursed with the exhaustion of one who has no place to lie down.

He was afraid to abandon his machine. It would be stripped. No radio to pass the time, he watched with his doors locked the night people passing who, he realized, had become morning people on their way to bus stops and work. The sin had all been sucked into the sewers. The dreamless people were emerging with lunch sacks.

Long after his hands had begun shivering with fatigue and his eyes had taken on the color of autumn, he walked six blocks to a small gas station at 20th and Blake and paid a mechanic five bucks to revive the Buick.

He drove with his back to a crucifying dawn up into North Denver. His brother passed on his way to work in his newly purchased 1964 Chevy. They both grinned and waved crazily.

The night had the disjointed atmosphere of a dream of death, and the morning light gave it all an incomprehensible distance. His apartment was filled with gray light. In the bathroom, he showered and prepared an ice-cold glass of water which he set on the floor in the dust next to his bed where it would be when he awoke from pale dreams of rivers swallowed which would not cool his tongue.

CHAPTER 7

Celeste was a senior at the University of Colorado at Boulder and would be delighted to see him again.

With the arrival of winter, he found the days as similar and numbing as the unchanging weather in the war which had made the year one long hot day with intervals of darkness, and his memory of the place was that of a long slow flickering silent film.

One evening Palmer peered into the bathroom mirror to see who was looking back at him. His face was not clean and shiny, like brass or polished boots. Dark circles under his eyes. A patch of jungle rot had appeared at his temple but then had faded as though unable to withstand exposure to light or public scrutiny. The rot had spread to his thighs, calves, arms, chest. The balm kept the disease from itching. His beard was thick now. His uncut hair covered his ears. He did not think his eyes would ever be white again.

It took a few phone calls. Celeste had the sort of parents who did not stay home nights. They were delighted to hear from him again. They did not know he was "back from the service." He had imagined everyone knew it. They gave him her phone number. She roomed with "a bunch of great gals" off-campus and would be delighted to hear from him. She was a history major.

On the Friday he was to go up to Boulder to see Celeste, he awoke from a hideous dream of spiders. In a poorly lit basement he scooted beneath low rafters from which hung tiny spider-like dangling hands, passed through curtains of them, brushed them from his body and knew all along it was a dream and remembered other agonizing dreams. He awoke with fists red and clenched, his eyes wet, and he threw the covers off his bed and walked around the room with his arms held away from his body until the mood of the dream evaporated.

The road to Boulder was dry. The tollbooth gates had been removed since he had last passed through Broomfield. The snow on the hilly fields was melting in curved irregular patches, yellow grass emerging. The temperature had risen and he was blind without sunglasses.

He was surprised at and disappointed in himself. Palms moist, the constricting throat which would not cease its rhythmic swallow, the heavy breathing. He was a child about to give a speech before a class of schoolmates he must, for five minutes, pretend not to hate. He sensed nothing had changed. He had been in Vietnam. That alone ought to have cured him of the petty social fears, but he was afraid she would discern no change in him at all.

Her disapproval haunted him. During the anxious months they had dated it never occurred to him to disapprove of her. Overwhelmed by the entangling presence of her body, bony and soft in front-seat wrestles, the perfume she wore in the beginning (before informing him he wasn't worth six dollars an ounce). Palmer's brother had attended CU, flunked out on poker and beer, and Palmer had spoken of Boulder with his friends as though it was an exotic, distant place where only the elite were allowed to dabble in its mythos. "Yeah, gotta run up to Boulder this afternoon and give Mike a cashier's check. Probably buy me some beer, might even sneak into Tulagi's. Yeah, gotta go guys. Gotta go up to Boulder" where all the coeds are trying out their pussies for the first time, where only the most brilliant novels are read and discussed. And he, young Palmer, not even of college age, fucking around with College Men while his lesser friends pick their noses in Denver and put new transmissions into their heaps.

Boulder had grown in spite of its laws. He got lost. The bar was on Pearl Street, he was an hour early. It gave him time enough to get a little drunk. She had never allowed herself to see him drunk back then. He chose a booth in the rear of the bar, a stiff-backed and awkward booth, but intimate. Their legs would clash throughout the meeting. She is engaged. He ordered a beer and a shot of Johnnie Walker Red.

Her hair had been long, straight and blonde, and she had kinetic blue eyes. When they looked at you they gave your heart a little orgasm.

She stood overexposed in the Boulder sunlight and then entered the doorway and became a silhouette moving toward his table. Familiar stride. He stayed an urge to knock back the shot. She kissed him and sat opposite and turned for a waitress.

She drank. He offered her a cigarette, now she smoked. Her hair is short and curled, almost a fro, gone is the lipstick of high school, but there is still something pink on her cheeks.

"You look fatter," she said, her fingers snaking across the table, "your face," touching his jaw.

"I put on weight in Vietnam," knocking back the shot. "I can't stay long," she said. "Dale and I are blowing off our history of England. God how I hate that teacher. I do not lie, I am waiting for the day when I am out of this place and do not have to worry about homework papers or reading. I swear to you, when I get out of this place I am never going to read another book as long as I live."

He smiled and ordered another shot. Already touched by the alcohol, he began to feel awkward, having never been drunk in her presence. "How's your schooling?"

Alice found herself walking away from the hilltop. He wished he had not asked that. She cared nothing for school, and neither did he.

"By the way," she said, "if anyone asks, if my parents ask, I'm still living with Pearl and Shirley. Dale and I have been living together for the past six months and I'm afraid my father will disown me."

He nodded. "Do you remember," he said, pinching the shot glass between thumb and forefinger, "that double-date we went on with Mathews? We went to the Cinerama and saw How the West Was Won." She licked her lips, puffed the cigarette and shook her head, no, she didn't.

"Afterwards we went out and parked at Cherry Creek reservoir. Do you remember that?"

She smiled, she was beautiful, but no, she couldn't remember. The doorway darkened and she looked as a man entered, but it was not Dale.

"I've been trying to call you ever since I got home but I couldn't get hold of you," Palmer said. It came out of his mouth in a quick timbre which made him uneasy.

"Really?" Blowing smoke down at the table as she crushed out her cigarette. "You should have called the student directory service."

He nodded. He was lying. "I've been thinking of going to school on the GI bill. How do you like it here?"

He wished he would not say these things. His underwear suddenly felt very tight and uncomfortable in the crotch and he concentrated on not moving.

"Please, let's not talk about this hole. I am so sick of school, believe you me, I am looking forward to the day when I have an eight-hour job, no homework and no term papers."

He smiled and when the smile did not go away he knew it was all over. He drank at his beer and with the glass held high, gazing at her through the warp, that feeling returned, that old feeling. He was suddenly buying time because he was in a place he did not wish to be.

He lit a fresh cigarette and inhaled deeply. "Do you remember . . ." He was about to ask if she remembered the drive-in movies he used to take her to, the ones she disliked so much. He grew embarrassed. Each sentence might now begin with the words Do You Remember.

"How was Vietnam?"

He looked up at her. "It wasn't so bad. I was in a relatively safe place on the coast. I never did see any real action. I had a desk job. I never was in any danger."

There was nothing false about the words, but he felt as if he had uttered a terrible lie.

"I always thought about writing to you," he began. He was closing in on it, it was there. For all the time they had gone together he could never actually remember saying anything to her. Juvenile poseur. "If I hadn't been drafted," he began again, except they broke up months before he was drafted. The doorway darkened and they both looked. "Do you remember the last time I talked to you?" he said. "After we broke up?"

Something said. He had never said that aloud before.

No, she didn't remember.

"I called you at one in the morning. Do you remember?"

She had that thoughtful look. She was trying to remember. "When was it?"

The month before you went to Boulder. "I was pretty drunk and I said some things I always wanted to apologize for. In fact, in Vietnam I started to write a couple letters just to apologize because I didn't want, you know, our relationship to have ended on such a sour note."

She shrugged and sipped at her drink. "I probably spaced it as soon as I hung up." She smiled. She was not being sarcastic.

He ordered another shot and asked if she remembered the time they went to Gates Planetarium on a Saturday afternoon in June.

"I remember you didn't want to go," she said.

"You remember something."

"You thought it was corny," she said. "You thought everything was uncool back then. I wanted to go bowling with friends and you wouldn't because bowling isn't cool."

He feels his ego shrinking. It's like a magician or a juggler who stacks up a tower of blocks and then, with one swift stroke of a small flat bat, knocks a single block from the middle and they all drop one notch. Yes, it's true, he was a snob back then. He was afraid James Bond might stop in at the Bowl-O-Rama to buy a pack of cigarettes and see him bowling.

"But don't you remember our double-date?"

She grinned and touched his arm. "Why are you talking about things that happened so long ago?"

He was mortified of course. Both of them looked at the darkening doorway, and Palmer hoped to God this was Dale coming in.

He remembered now. This was why they had broken up. Everything had been a mystery to him in those days. What he actually wanted was to say, Let's go up to your place and fuck. She was so beautiful. Soft lips, and those eyes; if only she was a mute.

"Dale, this is Palmer."

He was a fine-looking young man.

They would be married in the spring.

Afterwards he drove around Boulder because he had not seen it since his brother flunked out. Autumn had passed, the smell and colors, afternoon sun against unraked frat house lawns, were gone, the mythos of the university was not there. Somewhere there had been a small art cinema where he had seen the silent version of The Phantom of the Opera. He had been content then to stand outside the world of students and view it and never be a part of it because the mythos gave his heart little orgasms. It was strange. Celeste was exactly as he remembered her.

The road out of Boulder was empty and he accelerated up the first long turnpike hill and watched the needle on his speedometer fall. She had taken a number of courses in Human Sexuality. She had seen a documentary on Masturbation. He put the Buick in second gear but the needle continued to fall. He was being passed by Volkswagens. She quit shaving her legs a long time ago. She still wore a bra, though. They were going to have two children and then Dale was going to have a vasectomy. She'd been on the pill for the past three years and didn't want to risk blood clots. A friend had a clot pass through a lung which almost killed her. The Buick rolled over the top of the hill, and he left Boulder behind him forever.

He stopped at an unfamiliar bar in North Denver because he could not return to his apartment as if returning from a trip to the laundromat. Even though he was not shaken to the core by disillusionment, he wanted to give his emotions a chance, should they be too embarrassed to speak. Two or three shots of scotch. He felt the same now as he'd felt after dates where he had squirmed under the assumption he didn't understand her, that there was something beneath her surface. Minus the wet underwear, the sore cock. He went to an unfamiliar bar to see if he might get punched out by the regulars. It was a neighborhood bar and possibly had never seen a fight in its time. Whenever he entered an unfamiliar bar, he broke another illusory hymen. They were all run by old people. He didn't know what he was looking for.

He arrived at his apartment after the sun was down, and his drunken state of mind gave him no pleasure. He went to the closet where he removed his army uniform from the hanger and laid it out on his bed. The medals were missing.

He went back to the closet and searched the floor and found the ribbons in the laundry box. The ribbons had been washed. They looked like colorful shredded wheat. He pinned them back onto his uniform and stood back and remembered the day he bought the ribbons in Cam Ranh Bay just before coming home. They looked like shit. He put the uniform back into the closet and told himself to get a new set of ribbons, out at Lowry Air Base or Fitzsimons Army Hospital. He went to the refrigerator for another beer and remembered there was no more.

He was thinking about something so he drove right past the liquor store and had to double back. On the way home he wondered why it was that no one played Big Band music on the radio. He twisted the dial as he drove, but he did not live that far away and when he arrived he was not even halfway through all the dim and distant static sparks of music which burst and faded with the turn of the knob.

His brother came home at midnight, opened a beer and drank half of it and tried to watch TV, then collapsed into bed.

Palmer took the remaining beer from the icebox and turned off all the lights. He did not decide where he was going until the car was underway, and then he decided to go to Boulder to talk to Celeste. He did not realize how drunk he was until he found himself on north Federal passing the grounds of Regis High School, Mike had graduated from there. He didn't know what he was doing on north Federal, the road to Boulder was west. He had been driving and lifting cans to his lips and following old roads with no thought to where he was headed. He was no closer to Boulder than he had been when he was sitting in his apartment. He decided

not to go see Celeste after all. He stopped at what appeared
to be a cowboy bar in Westminster and went in for a shot.
There was a country band and two other people in the place
which was a large dancehall. He knocked back the shot and
left.

He drove down Federal south of Colfax and stopped in
at tacky little stucco bars on the main drag, and passed up a
joint encircled by silent gleaming Harley-Davidsons.

The same woman tended each bar—late forties, a Midwest
accent, you could tell she was a lady. A man poured a stein
of beer onto the head of a woman and the woman screeched
and ran to the restroom yelling "fuck you, fuck you." Palmer
left and bought a newspaper from a machine.

At a bar near Alameda he sat alone in a booth and saw
what he was looking for in a pretty and alone woman drinking margaritas at a table. He watched her for half an hour
until it was clear to him he was not going to approach her.
He paid his tab and left. Perhaps if he could leave her head
here and just take her body to a motel, that would be all right.

He turned on the inside light and propped the newspaper
against the steering wheel and turned to the classified ads.
Lucky Stars Escorts. French Encounters. Aphrodite Massage
Parlor. Oriental Expressions.

Further down Federal, he imagined it would be a well-lit
storefront, an abandoned barber shop renovated, but it was
a few blocks east of Federal, in a dark neighborhood, a small
redbrick duplex.

He had never yet encountered trouble finding a parking
space for his car which had no reverse. He stopped flush with
a driveway and shut off the engine and looked at the twin red

doors of the duplex. The only lights in the neighborhood, dim-watt bulbs over each door. Residential. He removed the keys and they fell from his hand and he slapped the floor blindly and when he found them he shoved them deep into a pants pocket.

He chose the door on the right and when he opened it he awakened an Asian woman asleep on a waiting-room couch. She lifted her head and smiled sleepily and he told her he would go next door. She nodded and lay back.

He entered the door on the left and a woman stepped from the back room wearing a sheer nightgown. How much for a nude massage? Twenty dollah.

She led him into a room filled with blinding red light but he shook his head. She took him to another room, white, clinical, antiseptic. A doctor's office, a doctor's examination table. She left the room while he removed his clothes. A mirror placed in an unusual position on the wall. Sumo wrestler bodyguard watching beyond, a well-armed eunuch, two fragile women could not run this den alone.

He lay on the cool disposable paper sheet and waited for her with his eyes closed. Twenty dollah. Money can substitute for anything. She entered and locked the door and removed the nightgown, big breasts, brown nipples bobbing. She wore shiny turquoise bikini panties. At the sink she filled her palms with oil.

He remained limp, suppressed his apprehension and watched her ass. She asked what the red patches on his body were. Jungle rot, he told her, from Vietnam. Are you Vietnam? he said. Chinese. She was a big woman. The women in Hue have hair on their pussies, Suzy had told him. Suzy's was bald. The woman scooped up his limp cock and it slipped like a peeled grape between her quick fingers. "It's only jungle rot," he said. She applied more oil, a hand on his chest as though she was working over an ironing board. He began to massage her breasts and she did not stop him.

As soon as Palmer walked out the front door he saw a police car roll down the street. He hesitated under the glare of the porch light, then walked to his car and got in and waited to see if the cop would return. Idle cops. He pulled out from the curb and stopped at the intersection but the law was not to be seen.

Federal was deserted. His beer was warm, but he wanted no more beer. He came down his street and did not want to go into his apartment and he drove past. There was no place he wanted to be.

West Colfax was a bright abandoned midway. He drove its length and turned back when the darkness of the country-side began to appear, drove back along the corridor of silent colored lights to a motel with a vacancy.

The night clerk watched him sign in with a guarded look. Palmer had to go check his license plate number. He took the key to his room, went inside and lay down in the clean silence, and fell asleep with the key in his hand.

CHAPTER 8

The map's legend referred to Denver as The Queen City of the Plains. It was stained with beer. His brother had come home and gone, he knew a woman with a condominium in Vail and would not be back for a day, two days. Palmer touched the browning wrinkles, still damp, his brother was a slob. He spread it out on the tabletop and lit a cigarette.

On the floor lay the want ads scattered, ashes of the night before when he bought a paper in a burst of enthusiasm to look not for a job but for an apartment. This dump was concrete around his feet. He had lost interest last night because it came to him in a flash of alcoholic insightfulness that whatever he needed, it was not a new place to live. He now felt his conclusion had been wrong. The worst problem he had ever encountered was solved neatly the day he climbed on that 727 and flew home. The only thing he does need is a new place to live.

He had drawn ink circles around placements and now wondered what he had been thinking. Expensive towers, it was a familiar ruse. Set goals so unrealistic that inertia kicked in and gave you an exit. He tossed the papers aside and began cleaning himself up. Nobody advertises in the papers. Landlords want the people who want it bad enough to get out and dig it up. Besides, he knew where he was headed anyway and it wasn't Englewood or Glendale, it was the heart of Capitol Hill.

He drove in unfamiliar cold daylight. It was overcast and a dry dust of snow blew along the streets. He took Speer

Boulevard and when he crossed Larimer Street at the bottom of the viaduct he resisted the urge to drive past that hotel. The destruction companies had leveled a square block along Cherry Creek, brick duplexes built before the word was conceived. He wondered momentarily why the streets were deserted and then remembered it was Christmas Day, and almost turned around to drive home because he doubted any landlords would be interrupting their celebrations for him.

He drove on, however, because there was nothing to go back to and he could browse the For Rent signs, bright red letters on black tucked away in dark windows. Fourteenth past the museum he would never visit, past the post art deco library where he could remember having gone only one time in his life, to look up "facts" for a high school debate, searching old issues of Time magazines and shitting his pants with excitement because he felt like such a fucking grown-up. He lost the debate.

Fourteenth cut straight across the hill and he wondered where that bar was, made up to lure the Tolkien fans with its dollar wall posters of Middle-earth and green beer. He had nibbled around the edges of the Youth Revolution, watched wide-eyed as long-haired hippies strode past with beads, Capitol Hill had smelled like a bag of pot, its odor now long gone. He had wanted to be a freak but ended up an MP.

At Colorado Boulevard, he turned back and threaded the side streets, crisscrossing Colfax until the purpose of his motion became Motion. He bought a hamburger at a new McDonald's near the Cathedral and drove down into the business district and began to realize what a truly tacky city this was. The smog wasn't new, he remembered seeing it when he was fool enough to pedal up Lookout Mountain on a bicycle, one gear, a J.C. Higgins. Old buildings boarded up, a dump on a civic scale, and he liked the fresh acres of asphalt flattening Larimer Street. A stilled wrecking-ball hung over a halved building. A third-story interior exposed, a closet door shut, he wondered how many derelicts had died among those peeling walls.

Up Seventeenth, he drove past the Centre Theatre at Broadway where again the grown-up memory blew out of the underground parking lot, such a grown-up place to park. He sipped the iced Coke empty and tossed it into the backseat. This was not a big town. Tall buildings sprang up, but for miles around low buildings and houses spread. If there were mountains to the east, this would be a desolate valley. The Broncos had lost another game. The war was lost. His high school had not claimed a single victory and he had graduated with the idea he was getting away from something.

He stopped at a light on Broadway and when it turned green he felt that inexorable inertia, there was no reason to accelerate. San Francisco, the Sears store on the top of the Geary Boulevard hill, a white, a pastel city with the rising metallic ocean all around. The faint odor of cigarettes on tarnished fingers. He decided to go back to his apartment, but first he drove back down to the Denver Bottoms, near Union Station where the new Ginn Mill had been established.

They wouldn't come in with him. They dropped him off at the corner and he entered the bar and took a booth in the dark, there were ancient boxing photos on the wall, black-and-white and autographed. The first drink came, no problem, it was past one o'clock and the bartender looked the other way. But two black-suited drunks were arguing at the bar in the smoky air, it looked like fisticuffs to Palmer, and he moved up to a bar stool, he would intervene and meld with them, he would become a regular in the night. But when his beer came he knocked it flooding to the counter and when the bartender demanded his I.D. he slipped off the stool and ran, ran out the door and down the block and laughed only when he was safe inside the car with his friends who asked what had happened, and he felt a universe away from them and would not answer.

The Ginn Mill was open for Christmas Day. Palmer drove past, then went on down the street and looked at the stained-glass tableau of the Oxford Hotel. Ortega had worked as a busboy at the Oxford, the Puerto Rican truck driver who was Palmer's first contact with the tragedy of innocence in a world of truck drivers who made themselves the heroes of barroom battles. Ortega once said that when he finally left home he kept looking out the airplane window for the place where Puerto Rico's air was connected to the United States' air, because he thought each place in the world had its own separate sky.

CHAPTER 9

It had snowed heavily the day after Christmas and each morning thereafter Palmer awoke and felt as though he was enclosed in a cave, peering out the windows through a circle of haze and dark snow against the pane. In one of the small tin kitchen cupboards he found a quart of Johnnie Walker Red which his brother had brought back from Vail.

With his breakfast of scrambled eggs and soda crackers he drank scotch, a thing which, even in the war, he had never done. He dressed only to go to the mailbox and pluck his unemployment check from the snowy lid. When the food ran low, he walked through the falling snow to the 7-Eleven and paid their high prices for canned food and white bread. His brother did not seem to mind about the disappearing scotch.

A few days before New Year's Eve, his brother came home with a fifth of Johnnie Walker and rather than go to a bar, as he usually did, his brother stayed home and read the paper at the table and drank. Palmer watched without interest the television and because he did not lack for money he felt compelled to feel grateful his brother was bringing in a steady supply from the liquor store, which was much farther away than Palmer preferred to walk. He felt, in fact, nervous with his brother around, and wished his brother would go away. But the snow had fallen deeper and they were both trapped in the apartment, and Palmer played his Glenn Miller record a few times, wishing he could play it the rest of the night, but he put it away because he felt it was annoying his brother, who heard nothing in Glenn Miller, even though his brother did not say anything about it.

Palmer had no more dreams of violence or death, but in his waking hours he began to believe he would never see the coming of the New Year, that he would never live to be twenty-three. He recognized it as the feeling which enshrouded him the entire time he was in Vietnam when he was certain he would never come home alive, even though he was not in a combat unit and was nowhere near the places where men were dying. He had feared mortar attacks which came every month or two, lobbed from the mountains near the city where he was stationed. Each night he had gone to sleep expecting to hear the sound of exploding rockets walking toward his barracks, each dawn he awoke with anger in his eyes.

On the morning of New Year's Eve, he awoke to find his brother up and dressing. There was to be a party that night and his brother was going to help set it up, and Palmer was more than welcome to come if he wanted. Palmer took down the address, not because he believed he would be going to the party but because he had developed a knee-jerk reaction against refusing to attend any sort of function, the attitude which had ruined his teenage years.

His brother left, and Palmer started to get up to mix himself a drink and keep the deadened tradition of the past week going, but instead he collapsed into a deep sleep and awoke after dark, hunger truly gnawing at his stomach.

The apartment was cold and he hurried to the gas heater to light it. He turned on all four stove burners and made himself a meal of eggs, and when that wasn't enough he made a hamburger and ate it to the tune of Glenn Miller.

He took a scalding shower and washed until he felt as tight and slick as a clean plate and the cold had been drawn from his bones. He dried his hair and dressed and felt fluffy, and when he mixed his first drink of the evening and it began to hit him, he suddenly felt the overwhelming desire to see and talk to people. He found the slip of paper with the address to his brother's party in the thick dust beneath his bed. The sky had been clear all day and some of the snow had melted and he was pleased to find the streets had been sanded and cleared of ice. When he climbed into his Buick and heard it start up smoothly he felt complete, with an inner satisfaction he had not known in months, and he placed the shift into gear and glided away from the curb with a small glass of scotch in his hand, no longer afraid he would never see the coming of the New Year.

They were playing board games. The dining room table was crowded with determined men who rolled their lettered dice and arranged words with fanatic concentration. He did not know any of them but after learning who the host was he introduced himself and was told his brother had gone off to another party but would probably be back later. He was invited into a game of poker but felt intimidated at his inability to remember the sequence of hands, and so declined. The game closed in on itself and he watched for a while and when he finally realized he was not a part of it, he wandered away and found he had nowhere to go but to the keg which sat in a bathtub full of ice in the bathroom where blurred strangers barked jokes and filled cups in the camaraderie of mechanical dexterity. There was something important about filling the cups properly.

For a while he became the one who filled the cups, reaching out for the proffered container, women, angle and no foam, handing it back for another, say funny things, but then there was nobody who wanted a beer and he filled his own again and left the bathroom when a woman wanted to use it.

He played the dice word game and won and wanted to continue playing, but two bickering men with dollars to bet were handed the dice for a grudge match. Palmer finally went into the living room where people sat along the walls, on couches and chairs, or on the floor alongside bookcases and potted plants, and for a bit he examined the meager album collection near the stereo where another man had taken charge of the music. He found an early Animals album and suggested they play "We've Gotta Get Out of This Place," but the man in charge set the album aside and said it wasn't the right sound for now.

Palmer went for another beer and then found the host and tried to be casual as he inquired whether his brother had made it back yet and the host said he hadn't. Palmer felt if only his brother were there to introduce him to one or two people he could ease into the party, disappear into it, perhaps even become a part of it.

He tried the red wine in tall bottles on the dining room table. There was no scotch. The wine mixed well with the beer and when it began to run low Palmer offered to go pick up more for the host, who gave him ten dollars and told him where the nearest liquor store was.

On the way back from the store, Palmer realized his mission was not of the essence, no one was impatiently awaiting his arrival. He looked for his brother's car along the street and when he did not see it he drove once around the block deciding. He parked his car and went into the party and walked past the host with an empty cup in his hand. The host said nothing. Palmer put a ten-dollar bill in a cupboard and left the party.

Twist-off caps, he drank at the wine on his way back home. There was a six-pack of beer in the icebox. All totaled, enough alcohol to get him, if not as far as San Francisco, certainly as far as Salt Lake City.

The note read, "I'm going to California. I will call you." Five minutes to find a broken pencil stub in a chest of drawers, an eraserless relic of a Putt-Putt golf course from tournaments lost. He wanted to write more, but had no words.

Two bottles of red wine on the seat, an open can of beer in his crotch, I-70 was illuminated on either side as he rose into the mountains past Golden. The car was warm, the heater blowing, a map lay on the floor, indecipherable. Only now did it occur to him the two men in the gas station might have wondered, might have even smirked, at his inquiry, "Do you have any maps to California?" An all-night filling station, New Year's Eve. He gassed up and left quickly, even now it was a blur, he had pulled out onto Colfax and did not realize the street was divided by a cement island. The crash of the car across its low surface had shocked him and for one moment he thought of returning to his apartment and forgetting it, but turning back always had been his curse. He hoped the gas tank had not been ruptured.

Safe in the boat, swaying up the mountain highway, Salt Lake City by daybreak, it could not be so far away. He opened and pulled at the wine, the windshield was like a movie screen. He hoped his brother would understand and not worry. A year in Vietnam, the worst was over. There can be no more worry. Watch for the signs. There was a northern turnoff around Idaho Springs. His brother had tried to call Vietnam one night from a bar. "My brother is an MP," but he could not remember where or with what unit. Palmer would have liked that, it would have been around nine in the morning, sitting at his desk, typing reports, a call from a bar in Denver from his brother just to talk, one o'clock in the night. "What are you doing?" Twelve thousand miles away. "Drinking!"

The road went downward and he took his foot off the accelerator and the shadows of the mountains rose about him. Deep in the danger of nature, safe in the Dynaflow. Watch for the signs. He had never thought of calling his brother. He wrote, but he could not come home for the funeral. He could not take an R&R, not to Hawaii or Bangkok, not even up to Da Nang or down to Saigon. Would not get on an airplane. Things coming at a bug in amber too fast. He would have liked to come home for the funeral. "Liked" in the way one can find peace in such a thing as that.

The exit came up quickly, he pulled to the right and passed through a tunnel and found himself on the road to Berthoud Pass. Should have brought some potato chips. Salt Lake City can be only a few hours off. He would find a motel and continue his journey at a slow pace. Just to get out of Denver, get away from that tacky place of such poor memories. Should have stayed in San Francisco, gotten a room somewhere in North Beach and never come back to Denver. To have just forgotten about it. There was nothing for him in Denver.

The base of Berthoud Pass, now it was a two-lane road, he began the upward ascent and was surprised such a major road should be two-lane. Once over Berthoud, Salt Lake City can only be a few hours' drive.

He threw an empty wine bottle out his window and the chill air swept over his face. He turned the heater up and opened another beer and the other wine bottle. The pines grew close to the road. The moonlight stark against the coming asphalt, he watched as each turn grew tighter. It must be past midnight, the New Year is here.

He had seen the patches of icy snow along both sides of the road as it grew higher, and he could see the glow of Denver to the east on the plains, and as the car rose higher and the angle of the road increased, the snow and ice crept out into the middle until the white line was covered, and for one moment he thought he should turn back. He was driving on a white road and still there were more and tighter turns ahead, and the pines were closer to the sides of the car.

He had taken a pull at the bottle and put its cap back on and was gliding up an icy stretch toward an extremely tight hairpin turn when the rear of the Buick seemed to simply twitch of its own volition and he found himself trying to wrest the steering wheel in the midst of a one-eighty turn, the wheels no longer a part of the road, the landscape moving slowly and wrongly past his windshield rather than toward it.

The rear of the Buick slid full thrust into the elbow crook of the hairpin turn, ploughing deeply and firmly into a snowbank which burst and scattered across the trunk.

He could barely remember having come up this road. Embedded in silence, he tried to think just what had caused the rear of the Buick to twitch, then gave it up in favor of finally realizing where he was and what he had done to himself.

He got out of the car into the numbing silence of the dark mountains and trudged to the rear and looked at the wheels sunk into the snow.

Back in the car, he fearfully placed it into gear and listened to the wheels spinning.

The engine off, the lights off, he looked at the vague silhouette of the treetops against the night sky. He had not passed a single car. He put it back into gear and tried rocking it without reverse. It bounced against the snowdrift and he could feel the wheels sinking.

He did not dislike it. He drank hard at the wine and took a drink of beer, got out and scraped the snow off the trunk with his arm, climbed behind the car and opened the trunk to search for any sort of shovel. He dug at the tires with the pointed end of a jack handle, and went to the car for more wine. He sweated in the cold, his coat unbuttoned, until each tire was cleared of burying snow, then threw the iron in the backseat, climbed in and gently placed the shift into Drive and felt the tires sink deeper.

He dug out again, then poked the point beneath the tires and found there was no firm bottom for either tire. He got back into the car and buttoned his coat and took a long drink of wine, turned the engine on and looked at the gas gauge. Hours left of idling time. The heater worked. That was the theme of mountain tragedy, newspaper thrills. Start and stop the engine with discretion in order to preserve gas. Someone would be along. There would be the State Patrol, and the blue-lighted snowplows cranking up each pass. Dawn was six or so hours off.

He let the engine run, idling, and he drank at the bottle of wine and sipped at the beer and his only clock was the gas needle slowly dropping toward the center of the gauge. The night in autumn when he visited the prostitute on Larimer Street and his battery had died. Waiting for dawn. He rolled the window down once to feel again the coldness of the mountain air, just to remind himself of where he was and what he had done to himself, and he wondered how far he was from the top of Berthoud Pass, and realized it was probably just as icy on the downside.

He thought it must be around five o'clock in the morning when, after the wine was gone and he was nursing the wiggling remains of his last beer in the bottom of its can, he finally admitted to himself that even if he did get pulled out of this ditch by some passing motorist or government machine, he was not going on to California. The motion of the falling needle, even more than the physical presence of the dark looming hillside masses, had taken the dream out of him. He would point the hood-ornament downhill and let the Buick carry him back to Denver. He knew now how far away Salt Lake City was, how far away everything was.

He had been told you cannot run away from things, and he had found that untrue. The most awful thing he had ever encountered had faded in the exhaust of jet engines.

The whitened top of Geary, electric trolley cars every five minutes, the sweet odor of saltwater and green leaves and sandy Sunset Beach. At the beginning of this journey he thought he would somehow find himself at that place in the morning. He put a wine bottle to his lips, but there was no wine left. He set the bottle on the floor and it tipped and rolled and stopped.

He held his beer can until it was empty and he tried to think about the things other than the things which can never be escaped, and all the time he kept promising himself that the one thing he would not do alone in the dark mountains was cry about it. It seemed to him finally the only thing he had any control over, and when it began, he found he could not stop it.

He wept until the morning light turned the road and the forest to red and then to gold as the sun lifted above the far plains and shrank, and the road and the snow between the trees grew white as burning phosphorus.

PART TWO

CHAPTER 1

On my way back to Denver from LA I stopped off at my brother's place in San Francisco and stayed a few days. My brother Mike runs an auto upholstery business that he started in 1976, during the summer of the 200th anniversary of America, the Bicentennial. I had visited him that summer too. I was there on the Fourth of July when thousands of ships and boats sailed beneath the red mass of the Golden Gate Bridge, gliding across its shadow and filling the same bay that my father had sailed out of without fanfare towards the South Pacific and the unknown in 1942.

I was asleep when all the celebrations took place. I watched them through a hangover on TV on the five o'clock news when I woke up. My brother was at work. He was organizing the inventory. He intended to specialize in tops. When Mike came home that night, we sat in the living room of his small apartment and drank beer and watched the video-taped repeats of the flotilla which graced the deadly waters of the bay lapping against the island where Alcatraz is poised, lone, businesslike, empty.

There was a thing I had always intended to do in San Francisco, but never did because I'd never had the time. Not having the time was one of my favorite excuses because it imbued my slightest whim with unfathomable significance. Deadlines were unconscionable irritants. Schedules were out the window. Brilliant people on the go don't live by clocks, their heels are jet-propelled, they leave vapor trails in the sky, you never see where they are, only where they've been. I never had the time. Time was smoke between my fingers. It was a bohemian concept and it was fitting that I'd never had the time to look up the haunts of the bohemians during those brief visits to San Francisco on summer break, spring break, or the time I quit college, abandoned my GI Bill income, and came to live with Mike for three months until he sat me down and asked me straight out when I was going to get a job.

"I don't have the time," I now imagine myself saying to him.

He wouldn't have bought that line because Mike is not much different than myself. We grew up together, one year apart, and knew each other well. But I was going to tour the city and visit landmarks made famous by the writings of the beats, the beatniks. I had the time now.

It was a Sunday morning when my plane from LA began circling San Francisco International Airport. The cabin was orange with morning light. Shadows swept at odd angles abruptly as the plane adjusted its flight path prior to landing. Passengers were waking up. They steadied themselves in the aisle, heading for the restroom to get rid of the scotch-and-soda and pops purchased on the flight up. It was cozy. Campers. The stewardesses stashed balloon pillows and blue blankets in overhead racks. Smokers lit up. I was in the smoking section, seated by the emergency-exit door. I was sitting in what would have been the center seat on the right side of the plane, except there was no far right seat. To my right was a metal well, and a lid which hid the emergency chute designed to pop out the door and allow crash survivors to slide to safety. It bothered me to be sitting next to it. I originally had been assigned to a seat at the very back of the plane, but a woman asked if I would switch seats with her husband so they could fly together. It was all right with the rational part of me, I trust planes even if I tell myself I don't, and also a plane crash is lethal no matter where you sit, don't kid yourself, don't talk about the famous last three rows that always make it through a crash. I grew up on those myths. The irrational part of me made a movie out of my situation. Even though I was through with movies, which is what I had told myself when I left LA, I still turned this subtle, innocent series of events into a death knell. The Main Character is asked to switch seats. During the flight, the emergency door breaks off and the Main Character is sucked into oblivion. UPI picks up the story, and the irony of his switched seat is broadcast across America, and for less than fifteen minutes I am famous for being a victim of ironic fate. Friends from high school tell their wives they once knew me. Tsk.

The landing was flawless, and I felt almost as good about being in San Francisco as I once had felt about being in LA, though San Francisco is a little too magic. I told my brother I did not think I could ever live permanently in San Francisco because I would be overwhelmed by its charm. Better to have a place like that set aside for visiting. A place where you can go once a year, feel melancholy, get drunk, and leave. The visits were always good. I had never had a bad visit to San Francisco, and although my visit to Los Angeles had been a bust, I noted as I stepped out of the terminal into the slightly chilled fog-lifted morning air that, still, LA had been even better, it owned me, because it was the movie capital of the world, and no matter how mesmerizing might be San Francisco balanced on those white hills with all its beatnik mythology, the legend of Los

Angeles towered over it, obliterated it, a surprising thing which I still do not understand, since LA is a very tacky and run-down place. Everywhere except in my heart.

I called Mike and told him I was in town, and he said come on over and don't wake him, he had been out late the previous evening. I had a key. I'd had a key since the Bicentennial when the whole world had paused to tip its hat in our direction and acknowledge what a swell country this is, even our enemies, who hate us because we've got it all.

Mike was asleep when I arrived. He was laying in a cocoon of sheets on his Murphy bed. His apartment is small, expensive west coast standard, it would go for less than two hundred in Denver but he pays more than five hundred a month, and when he is still there in ten years he will probably be paying a thousand a month. I put my duffel bag beside the couch and stepped into the kitchen to see what food he had. Thirty-three years old, one year older than me, and still living like a teen fresh from home. You go to a laundromat and put all your clothes into a single washer, whites and darks, God forbid you should waste more than a quarter on cleanliness, and if the clothes are still damp from the dryer, you hustle them home damp because they can dry wrinkled on hangers, God forbid you should waste an extra dime on ten more minutes of drying time, which I now read as "dignity" as I grow older. You shake your head with dismay at things that made perfect sense when you were a kid. Those dimes added up to a lot of six-packs of beer. I don't know what girls value when they leave home for the first time, but boys know exactly how much beer money they have in their pockets every second of the day.

A balled wad of hamburger in plastic which would be good maybe one more day. Two bottles of beer. In the cupboard spaghetti. I am home. My brother and I lived this way for years, ten years ago, so I felt like I had gone back in time, and felt a little lighter in my step, a little freer, irresponsibility has its good points. I left the apartment to go down to one of the Iranian-run grocery stores on the corner to buy food and maybe a jug of wine.

My brother's apartment is on a hill near the San Francisco State Medical College and the breeze from the ocean three miles west was rolling right up the street bringing a little fog with it. The sky was overcast, though I could have gone a dozen blocks east or north and seen high sun and blue sky. There was a grocery store on every block, Greeks kittycorner, Iranians kattycorner, the doors were open and I could see shelves of bottled wine running to the rear of the store, narrow aisles, wooden floors, it pleased me to think that these same warped boards were being walked upon by beatniks when I was a child in 1955. Old white freezers with rounded corners filled with scattered cartons of ice cream. Worn-out looking young men standing in a silent polite line at the cash register holding bottles of wine the color of coffee or lilac.

I bought some Mama Celeste pizzas, peanut butter, and a half gallon of pink chablis. I recognized the man behind the cash register who had been here when I visited San Francisco in 1976, a barrel-chested Iranian with salt-and-pepper Brillo hair leaning into his work, reading each item and ringing it up even though he must have had the store memorized and could probably tell you the price of each product since the day he'd fled his homeland and said this is it.

"Are you going to pay for that grape?"

A young man who might have been the owner's nephew entered the store dragging a man wearing a baggy suit, clutching his sleeve, a white-haired old man with a wine-shot face. "I caught this guy stealing a grape," the kid said.

There was a display of fruit set up outside on a cart.

"Are you going to pay for that grape?"

I picked up my sack and got out of there thinking what a cheapskate, and then, when I got to the top of the hill where my brother's apartment was, I thought I should have handed the kid a dime and paid for the grape myself. When I got into the foyer, I thought, stop thinking heroics. You aren't a hero and never will be. You couldn't even think of a way to help the guy, so continue to not think, bub.

Mike woke up about an hour after I got back. He pulled his pants on with his hangover groggy frown while I washed off the plate that had pizza on it. I'd saved a slice for him, but he didn't want it. He made a glass of ice water and sat on the couch and lit a cigarette.

"Did you get a movie contract?" he said.

"No."

He was the only one in the family whom I had told about the movie deal. I had come close to selling screenplays before but never as close as this, and even before I left Denver, when I had called Mike to let him know about it, I thought I might be jinxing it. But I'm not really superstitious, not like a man who plays the horses or dogs. I just need to think things like this to fix the blame because in the end nobody understands the real reasons Hollywood deals evaporate. They just do. Gone. So you make up a superstition. It happened because I told someone about it. If you're a Catholic, it happened because you told someone and God punished you for being presumptuous.

"I didn't find Strother Martin's grave, either."

My brother shook his head and exhaled a balloon of smoke. I saw words printed within its borders, "Too bad." That was the real bad news. He had never believed I was going to sell a screenplay, and in fact I didn't either. We grew up together. But there was nothing to stop me from finding Strother Martin's grave, except our family penchant for not succeeding at things that are almost impossible to fail at, which is to say, anything requiring minimum effort.

"Why didn't you find it?" he said.

"I didn't have the time."

CHAPTER 2

When you fly out of Denver west on a clear day, the mountains slide beneath you fast, runneled, rugged, it's like looking down at a topographic photo taken from a satellite. Plates of earth collided here, but slowly, shoving these plains into wrinkled rills, and look, there's the place where Alferd Packer ate his friends. I saw the glint of man-made things below as we sailed the mountains. I could see where highways had been cut, but Man's intrusion was now in its properly minuscule perspective. I looked straight down and tried to imagine pioneers crossing that slag in wagons with no roads. Give me the 20th Century any day.

There were no clouds when the plane came over Los Angeles. I don't think I saw any real clouds all week, just the haze which was new to me, and interesting. I tried not to be a rube. I had traveled to new cities in my youth, and something comes over you, you wrap yourself in the mythology of the hometown you hate. So this is San Francisco, Taos, Atlanta huh? Show me something. You gawk nevertheless. I remembered my father driving through new states on summer vacations, the family crammed into a Ford Fairlane, Nebraska, Missouri, I felt the eyes of all the natives fixed upon our license plate and I felt pugnacious. I felt this way because I had seen movies where new kids come to a new town and they have to fight the local thugs to become accepted. I pictured my father parking our car in front of a motel in some strange Midwestern state. A bunch of locals step out of a tavern and give us the eye, and suddenly my father has to fight one of them so that our family can spend the night in the Hi-Ho Motel on Highway 54. I was no older than seven. A lot of Mickey Rooney movies on TV in those days, black-and-white, a pugnacious kid. I thought life was like that. I jump out of the car and leap on the back of a local. "I'll help you, dad!" The fight peters out, the locals laugh, and someone hands my dad a beer and slaps him on the back.

Hollywood did this to me.

What I liked best was the sight of the Los Angeles river cutting straight across the city between the low buildings and houses. The sun was at a particular angle which turned the cement river into a ribbon of polished tin, and I imagined Los Angelenos a long time ago getting together and building a riverbed out of cement, straight as a picket-fence, a civic sculpture, then acting blasé about it. I sensed that there was a time difference of probably twenty years between LA and Denver. Denver was just now starting to look like the LA Jack Benny had cruised on his TV show. Bob Barker taking his camera out to Hollywood and Vine. Jack Bailey with his pitiful queens for a day. I had left Denver to make a three-point landing in the future.

I took a shuttle to a rental agency in an industrial area, it was like Commerce City north of Denver, factory buildings, smokestacks, grassy acres behind cyclone fences and concrete roads fanning out from the airport toward downtown. I rented a compact car with a seatbelt that wrapped itself around me like a robot when I got in. Good new rubber and plastic smell. I drove it up and down a few side streets, testing the brakes, steering, everything they say about driving in Los Angeles is true, I would find out. In such a mellow place, you have to stay alert.

I finally drove out into real traffic and gripped the steering wheel, reading signs and getting into the rhythm, and it came over me almost instantaneously: I could not get lost. It didn't matter how far out of the way I might accidentally drive, it was a physical impossibility to get lost in Los Angeles. There's an ocean on the left and those Hollywood hills up ahead, and more 7-Eleven stores than a man has a right to ask for. And how can a man get lost who's not going anywhere anyway? I was looking for a motel near the Farmer's Market, but in fact could have stopped at any motel I saw. Free as a breeze, I felt almost hypnotized in traffic, staying with the flow. I stared at everything because I had seen some of these things and places in movies black-and-white and color and now there they were, gliding past me, the big doughnut cafe, Sunset Boulevard, smog, I felt like I had come home, because this is where the Little Rascals had lived, this is where half my childhood was spent after my parents bought a TV. 1954. Watershed.

It was the Farmer's Market motel I went to, right across the street from Farmer's Market. It seemed a central location, based on the untutored observations I had made poring over maps of LA when I was still in Denver waiting for the day of my flight west to arrive. I have a friend in LA, Steve, who directs TV shows, and he was able to give me a general idea of how big and unwieldy LA is and the strategy of finding some sort of motel central to the activities you are planning. I wasn't going to Disneyland or Sea World, and I hadn't planned on going into the San Fernando Valley although I eventually spent an inordinate, and now that I think about it, an inexplicable amount of time there. Sherman Oaks. Tarzana.

Two times I got turned around and ended up back in Encino. It was eerie, like an episode of *The Twilight Zone.* I told the clerk I was staying for a week but he said there were no special rates for people staying more than one day. Fifty bucks a day. I didn't care. There was a movie deal afoot. My friend Steve had answering machines at his home and at his office, and I began leaving messages. He was editing a piece for broadcast television and had told me to get in touch when I arrived though it might be difficult for him to get away. The original editor had been fired by the network and now he was bearing the brunt, holed up in a small editing room for a week when I had called to tell him the news, and he said it could be a month before it was finished. A one-hour documentary. He had directed three-minute bits and half-hour spots and said he assumed this show would be easy, but now that he was deep into it he realized how truly long an hour could be when one is trying to fill up a cassette tape with images, some of which were only one-half second long. An hour's worth. Then the sound, narration, music. He told me to leave messages. If he could get away he would give me what he called the nickel-tour which he gave to all his friends who came out to see him and to see about scoring in Hollywood, he, among all our friends, who had gone out and actually had made it. I told him I was looking forward to the tour but what I wanted most to see was the walk of the stars. He laughed a native's laugh, and said it was actually called the "Walk of Fame," and that it wouldn't be difficult to see it. Then he asked me about the screenplay that was in my suitcase, two bound copies, just in case I might have to get down to business instantly and grind out a few changes, polish a few rough

spots. I had no idea how Hollywood really worked but I was
ready.

I was unpacking my suitcase and preparing to take a
shower when Steve called back, a punctilious fellow, taking
a break from editing. I told him I was going to call Fred's
office in the morning and let him and his agent know I was
in town and was prepared for a meeting. Steve told me good
luck and said to call him again the following afternoon, he
might be able to get away for a few hours, or maybe he and
his wife would take me out to dinner. He apologized again
for being in the middle of a difficult project with a cutthroat
deadline. I kept reassuring him it was all right, thrilled to be
allowed to paddle around the shores. Real Hollywood biz.

It was dark when I stepped out of my motel. I got into my
car and began driving through the balmy LA night weather,
just to throw myself into the crowd for a moment, to drive
Sunset Boulevard and Hollywood Boulevard, go with the traffic, not worry about parking, and view the glitter. A shooting
in East LA was reported on the radio. Drugs. I remembered
a movie I had seen at the Lake Shore Drive-In in Denver in
1966, *Riot on Sunset Strip*, about hippies and LSD and a cop's
daughter. I had sat in my car eating popcorn and watching
crowds of hippies massing on Sunset Strip. Hippies. Sunset
Strip. The movie wasn't about the plot, it was about this place,
and now here I was. It was a dream come true, just like when
I was sixteen and read Tolkien and wished I could visit
Middle-earth. I gunned my engine and looked at the hookers
and thought to myself, hooray for Hollywood, knowing that
if I ever revealed to anyone that I had thoughts like these I
would be drummed out of Hip forever. But I wasn't cool. I liked

it too much. I was no Albert Camus-Sartre-Belmondo cynic with a jaundiced frown. I looked into the rear-view mirror and saw a guy with a shit-eating grin driving my car, and I thought I must be the only guy in Hollywood not wearing a mask because I had a theory that everyone in Hollywood wears a shit-eating grin beneath his chosen make-up.

My screenplay was called *Cahoots*, a comedy I had written for a stand-up comic who shall remain "Fred" and whom I saw on a late-night variety show featuring up-and-coming comedians. Fred had a humble approach that charmed the audience. He communicated the sense that he knew things most people didn't know, but was not a threat, he was letting you in on the funny awful truths of life, like the young Woody Allen. I had been contemplating a new concept for months, ideas would come to me as I drove home from work, a screenplay which arose involving two women, they would be Americans around nineteen, and have fake French accents. I envisioned a buddy concept, Laurel and Hardy, except delightful, beautiful young women who get into wacky situations. Their names would be Babette and Gogi. I envisioned a series of Babette-and-Gogi films, like Gidget or Tammy, but with a slightly skewed reality, the characters becoming enmeshed in situations that bordered on puckish depravity. When I saw Fred on TV I thought he would make a perfect straight man for the first Babette and Gogi film, a known comedian whose movie would be the springboard vehicle for the B&G series. Fifty years from now people would say, "Oh yeah, whatever happened to Babette and Gogi? Did they have last names? Babette lives in a nursing home near San Rafael, and Gogi died five years ago in New Jersey. She owned a plant store.

People still called her Gogi even though her real name was Susan Buchanan. They pop up on the late show every now and then. They were voted the Sixth Fleet's favorite pin-up girls during World War Three."

Steve knew Fred's agent, and when I had discussed my idea with Steve he said the thing to do was go ahead and write the screenplay and he would see that Fred received a copy. The mysteries of Hollywood exposed: a screenplay is the easiest thing in the world to get to a star, a director, an agent, a producer, Southern California is hungry for good screenplays, they cut swaths through fields of bound manuscripts looking for the story which will earn them fifty million dollars at the box office. It makes sense to me.

I had written six screenplays, all of which had been read and turned down by Steve. All of them had been art, that is, message films, that is, non-commercial. The true nature of the form didn't jell until I actually sat down to conceive the first Babette-and-Gogi story and found myself writing a straight comedy with a plot, action, sex, adventure, and a good role for Fred, who took his sweet time responding after I sent it to Steve. The process is, you write a screenplay, you put it in a mailbox, you forget about it, you fish around for new ideas, you contemplate a legitimate career, perhaps in real estate, and find yourself one Sunday morning wiping toast across a plate of egg yellows and peering at want ads and wondering how unemployment could be so high when there are so many jobs available that you don't want.

Then the phone rings.

That's not part of the process. That's called "a fluke." You pick up the phone wondering who would be calling you on a Sunday, probably someone you owe money to.

"This is Fred. I'm calling about that screenplay you wrote. I like it very much. Could we get together for a meeting sometime soon?"

My brother told me his business wasn't doing very well and he was thinking about shutting down his shop and getting into some other line of work.

There had been a time when this announcement would have motivated me to at least act shocked. The history of our family had been a history of big deals. A flat tire was a calamity. Our lives were pitifully uneventful. I can look back now and kick myself for not appreciating the absolute vacuity of my childhood. It was almost as meaningless and uneventful as my adulthood, except I didn't have a job.

I had bought some Coke at the Iranian grocery, it was too early for beer, and I offered Mike one. He took it and we both drank that first cold Coke swallow and gazed at different walls and got our minds set for a potentially unbearable conversation.

"What are you going to do now?" Mike finally said.

"I'm going to tour all the beat landmarks at last."

"Are you still reading that old stuff?"

He used to say "old shit" but then I gave him a copy of *On the Road* which he found interesting, though it didn't stir anything inside him, not even the Denver episodes.

"No," I said.

Mike ate eggs for breakfast, then started reading a *Time* magazine. I gathered my dirty clothes and walked down the hill to a laundromat to wash the LA smog off my corduroys.

I had been traveling a thousand miles once a year to do my laundry in this place for more than a decade. The laundromat was well-kept, seemed always new, I never saw the person who collected coins and cleaned the washers and dryers and repaired the soap-box vending machines. Tacky plastic chairs lined the picture windows. I had once seen the street-comedy group Duck's Breath Mystery Theatre get off a trolley right outside the laundromat and trot across the street toward a row of gray apartment buildings where they must have been staying during their local gigs. I wanted to step outside the laundromat and yell "Duck's Breath!" and wave. They would glance around and smile. It would be chummy and understated. I didn't do it.

I washed my laundry, and on the way back up the hill to my brother's apartment I passed the locked doors of a small bookstore which sold both used paperbacks and contemporary books. I stepped up to the damp glass and looked into the store. Shelves of books, a new green wall-to-wall carpet. The very first time I visited that store, in 1979, I picked up a newly published copy of an anthology of short stories which I did not know had been distributed. I opened it. My name was in the table of contents. I looked down at my name and it looked back at me, we smiled at each other and I closed the book and felt pretty good. I looked at all the thousands of books on the shelves, the names of famous, classic authors, and there I was, on the shelves with them, tucked away in a sardine can. The only way I could have been more obscure was to not be there at all.

I had received a letter from the publisher one winter day in 1978. It was snowing and I had just awakened, as all writers awaken, a little before noon, and my first thought was to go down to the mailbox. Don't waste time getting dressed. It's a pain in the ass to put on pants but you have to. My slippers left footprints in the light frosting of snow on the wooden steps which led down to the mailbox. There was a single letter. I carried it back upstairs believing it to be an advertisement, but it wasn't. It was a fluke.

"Dear Mr. Palmer," it began. They were pleased to inform me that my short story had been chosen to be included in the upcoming edition of their anthology.

I stood there for about three minutes just staring at the letter. I finally ate breakfast, then called a former English professor to tell him the news, and then, like all writers, I went out to buy some beer for the big celebration. "Don't quit your day job," the professor advised me. I was back in the apartment before noon and drunk by one.

CHAPTER 3

The Farmer's Market maids had not knocked on my door yet. I could hear them talking out on the balcony, could hear the wheels of their carts rattling, buckets being set on concrete. They were speaking a foreign tongue, little women who would be Mexican, Vietnamese. I was smoking a cigarette and rereading the scribbled instructions that I had written down the last time I had talked to Fred. He had given me the number of his agent's office, the address, even directions on how to get there, which were meaningless to me, west on Sunset Boulevard toward Century City.

I hadn't had breakfast yet. I was drinking a Coke and smoking a cigarette in preparation for speaking to Fred's agent. I was excited, my stomach aching slightly with anticipation. The bound screenplay was on the bed next to me. I had reread it earlier. After waking up, showering, blow-drying, I sat on my bed and gave it one last critical read which I knew was suicidal because if I found even one glaring flaw I didn't have a type-writer to correct it. I had polished it since the version Fred had read. The shock of finding someone actually interested in my script caused me to reread and rewrite what probably should have been left alone. I had shortened and tightened sequences, trimmed excess dialogue, and added a few scenes that had evolved in my imagination in between the time I sent the copy to Fred and the moment he called. I sat on the bed and smoked and reread it, thinking, This is the version that will go to the screen.

I finally dialed the number of Fred's agent. A secretary answered and when I told her who I was she replied immediately that Fred's agent had left a message that our meeting had to be postponed until the following day. My heart stopped. My fingers got clammy. I told her that this would be fine. She said I was to call at one o'clock the following afternoon and Fred's agent would speak to me personally. I thanked her, smiles floating out of my mouth like moths. I wanted her to know I was not disappointed, that this delay was just a part of show biz, no prob.

I hung up and sat on the bed and kept looking at my wristwatch as if the hands might begin spinning and suddenly it would be one o'clock the following day. A maid began knocking. I got up and put the screenplay back into my suitcase and opened the door.

"Excuse me," she said. "I come back later."

I started to tell her it was no problem, that I was going to find a place to eat, she could come in and clean. But I stopped myself. LA was turning out to be the place where people do things later. I picked up my key from the dresser and a copy of an LA guidebook and stepped out onto the balcony. The maid was shoving her cart into the room next to mine. I went downstairs, walked past the empty swimming pool, and climbed into my robo-car.

When the left-turn arrow snaps to red, at least two and sometimes three cars continue through the intersection, briefly blocking accelerating traffic. This became the Big

Danger Moment in my driving. I went north to Hollywood Boulevard and as long as I stayed in the flow, the traffic didn't seem much different than Denver's. I looked at the people walking past the Chinese Theatre, past newspapers blowing in the gutter. I drove east gawking. Lots of movie poster souvenir shops. I had been told there were two good bookstores somewhere along here. I went up a side street and circled around to make the drive back along Hollywood Boulevard. I saw the bookstore, and saw a parking space in front. I wheeled in, a compact car, amazed that I had found a parking space so easily. Maybe I had LA confused with the myth of New York City where there are supposedly no empty parking spaces. I would sort it out later.

The bookstore was a mecca of technical references. There were at least three new books on how to write screenplays. I thumbed them wondering if I ought to buy at least one, not only for the information but because it would be a book bought in Hollywood. A cashier sat on a wooden chair on a slightly raised platform, and I wondered if he enjoyed a legend. Did everyone know him, did aspiring young directors solicit recommendations: which book will turn me into Hitchcock?

I walked out without buying anything and found a slip of paper on my windshield, a flyer, but this had a photo of a beautiful girl with her butt shoved into the lens, Strip-O-Grams, call this number, it was almost pornographic and served to remind me that I was no longer in Denver. I tried not to be a rube, but innocence sees things. I want to see things.

The walk of the stars. It was there underfoot, brass-rimmed with names I knew. I walked with my head bowed reading and thinking that there was a small celebration and a sort of coming-out party for this one and this one and this one . . . I saw other people looking down at the stars. I saw the names of people I had never heard of in my life. The procession stopped at intersections and picked up on the next curb beyond honking cars. I saw Humphrey Bogart's star. I saw Bert Lahr's. I wondered if there was a book with a list of all the stars and their stars.

When I got back to my car there were ten minutes left on the parking meter so I unfolded my big tourist map of LA and located myself. A dot in Bic ink. If I went west for a long ways I would pass Beverly Hills, UCLA, Westwood, keep going, soon I would be at the Santa Monica Pier. North were the Hollywood Hills, green and plugged with houses. Steve told me to flat stay out of East LA. I told him there were historic places located in East LA, places filmed by D.W. Griffith, quiet residential side streets where Buster Keaton and Laurel and Hardy had shot movies. Flat fucking don't go to East LA, especially late at night, he told me. I felt East LA a-calling but I took his advice. He had lived here for more than eight years. A long time to live here, some would say. He would know. A friendly native.

I drove to Westwood and parked on a curved street near a hot-dog cafe and got out to look at the theatres where films were routinely premiered. *American Graffiti* first shown here, I had thought Westwood was a small town like Ogallala, Nebraska, out in the boonies where a film producer could get a slice of rock-ribbed American opinion. I thought a lot of things before I came to LA. I went into a restaurant and sat at an outdoor table on a rear patio walled with a tall white fence and ate a tuna fish sandwich that cost seven dollars.

I leafed through my LA guidebook at the table feeling as if I was being looked at, *Look at him, he's reading an LA guidebook, he must not be from LA, sheesh.* I knew that Strother Martin had been buried in Forest Lawn from reading a *Rolling Stone* article in which Bill Murray and Warren Oates went to his grave drunk and poured booze on it, fitting gesture. I was in San Francisco when the death of Strother Martin was announced on TV in 1980. I was drunk on red wine. News item. It wasn't a flash or a bulletin, just a news item. "Character actor Strother Martin died last night of a heart attack." JFK, Elvis, John Lennon, Strother Martin, I am one of the few people in America who knows exactly where he was at the moment he heard that each of those men had died.

"Strother Martin once said his favorite role was to play desert scum who fights like hell for the big break, and then blows it," the announcer said.

I was drunk so I picked up a pen and wrote those words down because I thought I would not remember them, but I have never forgotten them. I had a friend in Denver to whom those words would mean something. A Strother fan. When I got back to Denver I brought up Strother's death while we were in a bar. He thought I was kidding because he didn't know Strother had died. It was an awful moment for me, and then for him.

It turns out there are four Forest Lawns in LA, and they do not make public the location of the inhabitants.

I left the restaurant thinking I needed to find a quick way to locate his grave, I did not have time to visit four Forest Lawns. I had too much to see and do. This was my week in

LA, and thirty-two years of loose connections had to be spliced together. I especially wanted to see the La Brea Tar Pits.

I called Steve when I got back to the motel, both his home and his office. I left a message on his machines and mentioned that Fred's agent's secretary had told me to call back tomorrow. I felt my throat constricting as I related this unexpected twist. I hung up quickly. It's too stressful to talk to answering machines.

That night I sat on my neatly made bed and smoked cigarettes and drank beer and read *Variety* and *The Hollywood Reporter*, then leafed through a Sunday edition of the *Los Angeles Times* that I had been lugging around for two days. Just reading this stuff made me feel like I was a part of show biz. I had felt intoxicated from the moment I had gotten off the plane. I kept saying to myself, I'm in Los Angeles, and I thought about Jack Benny again, and started browsing the LA guidebook, and finally got out a map of the San Fernando Valley and studied the streets because Steve had told me that, for a newcomer without the cash, the San Fernando Valley was probably the best place to look for a first house. You move up as the good jobs and pay come. He was living in a place that cost six fat figures, he had paid his dues, he was living the life.

I read the names, Golden State Freeway, Topanga Canyon, Laurel Canyon, it made me giggle, there they were, place-names from Middle-earth, here's the canyon road leading to the house where Superman killed himself. Here's the Manson massacre. Here's where Montgomery Clift hit a telephone pole and ruined his face forever. And somewhere over here, in this maze of streets like a plate of spaghetti, is the Clampett house. All right there on a buck map and outside my window too. My thoughts drifted across the LA basin. Would Linda Blair give me an autograph? Why did Leo Gorcey have to die? And then, in the classifieds of the *Times*, a big, six-inch advertisement that said "Be A Game Show Contestant, Win Big Bucks Playing Jeopardy!" I didn't ever want to go back to Denver again.

It was a house house, the kind of structure a little kid would draw, a square box, triangle roof, and painted brown. It was in the middle of a narrow street which was almost an alley, a surreal San Francisco alley blasted white with sunlight and very clean. It was a house where Jack Kerouac had worked on one of the versions of *On the Road*, where he had once lived with Carolyn and Neal Cassady. There was no one in the alley, it was quiet and I felt guilty and stayed long enough only to double-check the address and take a photograph with my Instamatic. Even then I had a hard time believing it was the right house because the house in my imagination, from my readings, was old and gray, North Beach weatherworn, decrepit, and in fact I expected it to have been torn down long ago.

I went out of the alley and got on a bus and rode it to Market Street. I stood near the Woolworth building and looked at my map of San Francisco decorated with Bic dots. There was a hotel south of Market at Third and Howard where Jack Kerouac had stayed sometimes, and a bar where he sometimes drank when he was in town, and not far away was the warehouse where Ken Kesey and his Pranksters had hung out, which I had read about in *Electric Kool-Aid Acid Test.* Neal Cassady toyed with a small sledgehammer. All of my research had been done when I was still in college and discovering the beats following the paperback publication of Kerouac's first biography. I came across it at a 7-Eleven one night, after midnight. I had gone there specifically to find something to read and I spun the rack and saw his name and remembered it vaguely from a mocking review by a Denver Post critic who despaired that Kerouac was back to infect a new generation with his typing. I went around for weeks telling my friends about this writer I had discovered named "Ker-ook." Jack Kerook. I was finally corrected politely by an English professor at the University of Colorado at Denver who was French-Canadian and who found my interest in Kerouac charming because he himself had discovered Kerouac in 1957 when he was a troubled teen (Kerouac was a French Canadian too, a Canuck connection). Then I corrected a friend who pronounced it "Karroway." And then there was a man I met in a bar who pronounced it "Ker-O-Vac," like the battery. Jack Kerouac. The most mispronounced name in American letters.

The hotel on Third and Howard had been torn down. I walked around hoping I was mistaken, but it was all gone. There was nothing left to photograph, so I took a picture of the dovetailed street signs, then walked until I came to the Kesey warehouse. It was the right address as far as I was able to tell, but it did not at all resemble the warehouse described by Tom Wolfe. I walked up and down the block. The building had been painted recently, San Francisco pink pastel, and looked very tidy. I decided it couldn't be the right place but I took a picture of it anyway. Then I saw a single empty wine bottle lying on its side in an otherwise spotless gutter, and I thought, Bohemia at last.

CHAPTER 4

I awoke at nine a.m. and could not get back to sleep even though I was groggy. I kept thinking about the telephone call I was going to make at one o'clock. I got up and showered, left the motel at ten o'clock and drove to a hamburger stand on La Brea. It was not a McDonald's or a franchise, it was a one-of-a-kind hamburger place, they were everywhere, and the hamburger was thick and greasy and I could eat only half of it. It was ten-thirty when I drove up to Sunset Boulevard and turned west toward the beach. I drove slowly with the traffic, listening to the radio and trying not to think about the time.

I had a list of addresses I had put together the previous evening of comic-book stores in LA, and half of them were in Santa Monica. There was an underground comic I had promised my Strother friend that I would look for if I ever got to a big city, LA or New York. It was the sort of comic you would never find in Denver except as a fluke, a collection of comics in one big volume. My friend had lost his volume, and accused me of stealing it or losing it drunk, but I denied it though I easily could have done both. I drove the streets of Santa Monica peering at storefronts and noting parking places because I was not going shopping that morning, I just wanted to locate the stores so I could get to them easily when I had the time.

I drove back east toward downtown LA, this had taken only an hour, and I was in my motel room laying on my bed and smoking cigarettes at eleven forty-five. The maid had come and gone, the bed was made, the floor vacuumed. There was a pristine quality that shimmered off the curtains, and an odor in the air of immaculate cleanliness which buoyed my spirits. I began to understand the luxury of servants. It would be okay to be Charles Foster Kane.

At one minute to one I practiced dialing the phone and clearing my throat. "This is, this is, hem, hah, this is . . ." At one o'clock I dialed, and the secretary from the day before answered. She put me on hold and I sat carved in soap on my bed.

"Yes," a deep, drawn-out, friendly, masculine voice.

"This is Mr. Palmer," I said.

"Yes, how are you doing?"

"Fine."

"I'm glad you called," he said. "Now, if this is going to be a problem, let me know. Fred told me to ask you if it would be all right if we postponed our meeting until Friday."

I reached for my pack of cigarettes and began shaking one out.

"Till Friday?" I said.

"Fred said to tell you that if it's a problem, or if you would like to talk to him about it personally, you can get in touch with him this afternoon around three o'clock."

"It's no problem," I said. I didn't want to sound pushy, desperate, panic-stricken, at wit's end.

"Great. Fred wants to meet at two o'clock on Friday afternoon here at my office. Will that work for you?"

"Yes."

"Great. Why don't you give me a number where I can reach you."

I looked at the phone and recited the number printed above the buttons.

"Great. I'll see you on Friday," he said.

I hung up. I could feel adrenaline evaporating off my misty flesh. I sat there for a full minute unable to put together a single thought. Then I looked down at the bed. There were fourteen cigarettes lying on the bedspread. There should have been fifteen, but one was stuck at an angle inside the rattling pack which I was still shaking with my disembodied right hand.

Steve called me an hour later and told me he would like to take me to dinner that evening. He had married recently and wanted to introduce me to his wife, and to make up for his absence during my visit. I told him I'd like to have dinner. Perhaps noting something odd in my voice, he asked if anything was wrong.

"Fred postponed our meeting until Friday."

"Hmmm." Steve mulled it over, then told me he had assumed we'd already had our meeting, and in fact he had been looking forward to discussing the outcome, whichever way it went. He didn't say so, but I got the sense that this evening's eat could have been as much a dinner of condolence as celebration.

"We'll pick you up at six-thirty," he said, and we rang off.

I opened my suitcase and pulled out my copy of *Cahoots*. I sat on the bed smoking cigarettes and leafing through the pages, reading the jokes and punchlines which now, to my wary eyes, seemed leaden and overwritten. I took out my pen and held it over this and that sentence, wanting to cut or rewrite, but it seemed futile. Nothing I could do to the script could alter the fact that the meeting I had expected to attend yesterday was receding before me like a mirage, nor could it alter the fact that it made me feel rather shitty. My head felt hollow. I closed the screenplay and turned on the TV and sat on my bed for another forty-five minutes, getting up to switch channels now and then, expecting at any moment to hear a whooping howl of brass and a crystal-clear voice croon, "Welcome to the Babette and Gogi Show!"

I could not help but think that already my script was in the hands of a coterie of producers ensconced on a rocky height so unscalable that my name would be nothing to them but a flea's fart carried away by the winds of ill fortune. I finally got off the bed and shut off the TV and walked out of the room. It was only four-thirty and I had two hours to kill before dinner. In fact, I had three days to kill. This was Tuesday. There was Wednesday and Thursday to endure, and then Friday, and they seemed like three wooden walls upright before me on a benevolent obstacle course. I was getting a headache. I got into my car and drove out into traffic, went east to La Brea with a vague notion of looking for the tar pits, but finally ended up cruising the quiet palm-stitched lanes of Beverly Hills. It was there that I encountered The Map Man.

The roads in that part of town wind up and around hills heavy with greenery, thick-leafed trees and low shrubbery that drips down stone and brick walls. The sign upright on the ground was made of cardboard, "Maps To The Movie Stars' Homes," and there was a well-dressed Mexican boy of about fourteen waving and smiling at traffic. He didn't have the maps, he was just a shill, pointing toward the street where the maps could be bought. I hung a quick right out of the four-lane traffic onto a narrow asphalt street which slithered up a hill walled in brick on one side, bushes on the other.

Halfway up the hill, seated on a green-and-white lawn chair beneath the shade of a tree growing on the other side of the wall, branches extending out almost to the road, was the map man, talking to two women.

There was no traffic, it seemed almost like an alley but was a thoroughfare for Beverly residents. I pulled off to the right, parked and got out. The women were from Germany, they had chilling accents and were built like small sensual halfbacks with pretty faces. They were laughing because the map man was flirting with them. He looked about sixty-five and was talking fast.

"One more thing," he said, holding up a finger, then plucking a map from one of the fräulein's hands. "One more thing. Cary Grant lived at the end of this drive, right down the block from ZaSu Pitts." He was making circles on the map with a yellow felt-tip marker. I watched his quick hands.

"We haf to go," they said. They sounded like Arnold Schwarzenegger.

"And don't forget to drive by Errol Flynn's house," the map man said, and as he spoke he was already digging into a small pouch at his side filled with maps. He was getting my map ready.

I had seen Sally Fields do this in a film, was it *Gidget*, the TV show? And Tatum O'Neal did this in *The Bad News Bears*.

The women crossed the road to their car.

"Do you know where Strother Martin is buried?" I said right off.

The map man squinted up at me and hesitated, then shook his head no. A van drove up and parked across the road and a woman got out. The map man spread his map of

Beverly Hills on his lap and made an X on one of the spaghetti roads. "We are located right here," he said.

The woman came up to us, she was wearing sunglasses and a floppy hat, and pink pants that in another era might have been called pedal-pushers.

"Ed, do ya got any extra maps?" she said.

"No, I got no extras."

"We sold out fifteen minutes ago," she said.

"I'm almost sold out," Ed the map man said.

"I checked with Walter and he doesn't have any extras, and do you know what else? They run Walter off."

"Again? The bastards."

"Can you give me ten?" the woman said.

Ed looked down at his pouch, reached in and began fingering his cache of maps.

"I'll make it up to you tomorrow," the woman said.

It all sounded very important and businesslike and crucial, like people at a coal mine cave-in trying to round up hot coffee for the rescue team. Joel McCrea is going down into the hole without an air tank even though the foreman is worried about gas in the caves, but damnit there's twelve men down there clawing their way to the surface.

"I can give you seven maps," Ed said.

The woman reached behind her back and thumbed an itch, then nodded. "I sure could use ten, though."

Ed shrugged in his T-shirt and shook his head. "I'm running low," he said.

The woman took the maps and turned to go, then looked back. "The police gave me a warning. You watch out for them."

"They already run me off the main drag," Ed said. "What

do you think I'm doing up here? I got Manuel down on the corner standing lookout."

"All right," the woman said, waving the maps and rushing across the road to her van. Gotta get going. No time to lose.

"I don't understand why the police hassle us," Ed said, flattening the folds in the map on his lap. "We're good for the community, good PR. We tried to organize a couple years ago to make it legal to sell maps on the roadside. For crying out loud, tourists want to know where the stars live. The authorities get on our backs about every three months. You can't sell anything on the streets of Beverly Hills, but for crying out loud, people want maps."

"I want a map," I said.

"There you go, that's what I'm talking about," Ed said. "Here we are." He tapped a yellow dot. "Right up the road is Glenn Ford's home."

"Where did Jack Benny live?"

"Jack Benny, he was a hell of a man. Right here." He made an X on the map.

Two more cars came up the drive and parked behind mine. Three men and two women came across the road carrying cameras. Ed was circling and underlining addresses, and reciting famous names. One of the women lifted her camera to take our picture. Ed looked up and grinned, frozen, and after she clicked he autographed my map and handed it to me.

"Where did the Beverly Hillbillies live?" I said.

"Right up the road." He took my map and poked his finger into the spaghetti. "Here. They only used the house for the credits though. They didn't film there."

When I left, Ed was saying the same things he had said to

me and had been saying to the Germans when I arrived, and had been mouthing for God knows how many contented years. I heard him tell the new people that he had been a guest on Johnny, Merv, Steve, Parr, and Godfrey.

The Clampett mansion was on a curving, sloping street so toylike that it defied my preconceptions of how the rich ought to live. Beverly Hills and Bel Air seemed crowded, squeezed together, the roads as tiny as in a cloying dream. I slowed as I passed the Beverly Hillbillies' house. The driveway did not seem as long and elegant as I remembered from the TV show. Movies, ho hum, how they distort reality. But the facade was just as I remembered it. *The Beverly Hillbillies* was syndicated in Denver on an independent channel at two in the morning, but I hadn't seen an episode for at least seven years. When I was a boy I thought the show was hilarious, and then when I grew older, and the Sixties ripened and my hair got long, I thought the show was the bottom of the barrel of bourgeois anti-intellectualism. The only thing missing, I now realized, was Strother Martin. As I drove back down off the mountain I wondered if Strother might have appeared as a guest in some episode. Shady cousin from the hills arrives in LA to swindle his blood kin. I would have to start watching that show again.

At six-thirty Steve drove into the motel parking lot. I was waiting with my coat draped over my arm even though it was a little chilly, but not Denver chilly.

"This is Sarah," he said. She was a producer at the same studio he worked for. It had been a shipboard romance. I climbed into the backseat, and Steve drove. He told me there was a great Mexican restaurant in the Valley. We went up Laurel Canyon, a curving road that seemed strange and dangerous in the total darkness. The sky was overcast and the road was wet and there were no lights but headlights coming toward us. The radio was on and an announcer said five black youths had been gunned down in East LA. Steve turned the radio off.

"Two friends are meeting us there," Steve said. "Frank and Cynthia." Frank had been cast in one of Steve's films. Cynthia was his wife, a script supervisor for another studio. I basked in it all, show biz folks, these weren't the people I knew in Denver, carpenters, garage mechanics, waiters, people just like me, some unemployed. These people were part of The Industry.

The outside of the restaurant was pale adobe, I didn't get a very good look at it. We got out beneath a green canopy at the door and an attendant took the car and we went in. Steve's friends had not yet arrived and our reserved table was not empty yet, we were early, so we got Canadian beers and drank them standing at the end of the crowded bar. It was very small and cozy, and we tilted beers in each other's faces while Steve asked me how Denver was.

"I'm here, aren't I?" I said.

I wondered if this was a place people went to be seen, though it was too dark to see much of anything. Frank and Cynthia arrived and Steve introduced us. They were his friends from the old days when everyone was young and broke and didn't care. We got a big table in a corner in the dining alcove and Frank and Cynthia produced two wrapped boxes, wedding presents. We ordered smothered burritos, and when we were finished Frank asked if I had come to Hollywood to cut a deal with Steve for a feature.

"I'm supposed to have a meeting Friday with Fred," I told him. Their interest and excitement was inversely proportional to mine. They asked me about the history of the script and I felt less and less like talking about it. It was like talking about a UFO sighting. You ultimately would rather not. After the beer got to us, Cynthia and Frank and I began cracking jokes about how we missed each other and should write more often. It was like a college reunion. Everyone at the table was young and in love with success. Steve paid for the dinners, and when we left there was a damp wind blowing.

"Nice meeting you," Frank and Cynthia said. We shook hands all around and I got into Steve's car and sat in the backseat putting my coat on while they said their good-byes. I now think we were somewhere in Sherman Oaks but I couldn't see anything, and even when I did get to Sherman Oaks I didn't recognize anything and couldn't have recognized this place if I saw it. It was as if Steve had driven up Laurel Canyon into a crack in the side of the mountain, into a cave and a place where everyone sat wearing fuzzy sweaters and drinking Canadian beers and talking softly over candles in red cups, everyone young and in love with success and unbelievably pleasant.

On the ride back through the Hollywood Hills I told Steve I was interested in looking at apartments. We spent the rest of the ride talking about housing strategies and the first places where Steve had lived eight years previously, when he had come to LA with nothing but a demo reel and a dream.

★ ★ ★

I left my brother's apartment and walked down a brick San Francisco hill and waited for a trolley which would take me to Market Street. We passed Kezar Stadium on the way. Dirty Harry tortured the best criminal ever there in the soft green football grass. We passed the clinic on Stanyan Street where hippies vomited in an NBC White Paper episode, and where the best criminal ever staggered in with a knife wound in his leg, Hollywood blood dried on his pants, fire-engine red like a crazy woman's lipstick. I got up and asked the driver if I could make a connection that would take me to Union Square and he said yes. I asked for a transfer but he refused. I was supposed to have asked for it when I got on. I sat down thinking this must be like the rules in LA—whenever a pedestrian steps into the road, traffic on both sides of the road for fifty miles in both directions has to stop. Then the bus driver ripped off a transfer and gave it to me. He was teaching me a lesson, I suppose. Mass-transit etiquette.

I got off the bus onto a wide filthy sidewalk on Market Street in front of a Western Union office where I once paid twelve dollars to have sixty dollars wired to me from Denver. On that day I asked the woman what time they closed. "Vee nefer closse," she said, another Arnold Schwarzenegger.

I stood in front of the office examining my San Francisco tour guide map until two kids, a boy and a girl in their early twenties, who might once have been called hippies but were now just raggedy-ass kids, asked me for a dime, then a dollar, then hung around and told me what a nice coat I was wearing. They thought I was a street person only because I look like one.

I have long hair and my clothes are worn by time. In another era I would have been mistaken for a hippie, and in an earlier era a beatnik, and I am neither. I would more than willingly engage in commercial writing in exchange for a few hundred thousand bucks. In college I had thought I possessed ideals. This was in the mid-Seventies when practically everybody at least pretended to have them. I had read Jerry Rubin and Jack Kerouac, but when push came to shove, I saw screenplays as a lucrative source of income. The real me emerged from my bongo pad. End result? I'm standing on a filthy street looking like a raggedy-ass thirty-two-year-old hippie, with no sale in LA and a map in my hand that might take me to the places where once lived people who, if nothing else, probably were artists.

The transfer trolley took me up Columbus Avenue, and I got off across the street from City Lights bookstore. I walked down the block looking back at it, then crossed the street and walked toward it feeling embarrassed that everyone knew I was a beatnik fan looking for famous places. "Look Martha. Look at that white middle-class paranoid going into City Lights."

It had been remodeled, a wall knocked down and expanded into the storefront adjacent. If it ever had possessed the taint and odor of rebellion, a conclave of the seditious, that had been replaced by ferns and subtle lighting and varnished shelves of the latest best fiction and non-fiction that could be offered by any genial businessman. I was disappointed but not surprised. You can't run a successful business for thirty years by running full-tilt in opposition to society's cold-blooded pursuit of money. Though you might make a successful posthumous literary career embracing that tack.

In the brick-walled basement of the shop, redbrick walls, clean redbrick walls, I found a copy of *Scattered Poems* by Jack Kerouac who was gazing out from the cover in a black-and-white fuzz-grained photo looking like a worried, cap-headed Jack London. I decided to buy it. It would be a souvenir, even though the volume hadn't been published during his lifetime. I had read somewhere that Kerouac always had difficulty persuading Ferlinghetti to publish his poems, and that a lot of serious poets didn't consider Kerouac to be a true poet in the most virginal and thunder-hearted sense of the holy and sacred word Poet. It must have been easy, back in the Fifties, with all his success, his lionization by the media, and his worship by a generation of apostles, to be deeply envious of Kerouac.

CHAPTER 5

When I awoke Wednesday morning I was buoyed by the sense that the two days ahead of me were not at all an endless wait in an employment line but an opportunity to map out my future and begin pounding the stakes that would mark the boundaries of my career, and that it would all begin somewhere in The Valley. Without the bucks, you start in The Valley, Steve had told me, and somehow, through talent and luck, like pioneers you make that trek over the Hollywood Hills and down into West LA and carve out one of those six-figure cabins and then seven figures and so on. But it all starts in The Valley which I knew nothing about except wisecracks by stand-up comics which said the San Fernando Valley was where the squares lived or the dweebs or the plastic phony air-head nobodies, I couldn't quite remember what it was about the San Fernando Valley that was supposed to offend me, but I did know one thing: it sounded a lot like Denver.

At noon I took the Hollywood Freeway because it went up and over Cahuenga Pass, an event almost impossible to notice in a fast car, but I had seen a photograph of the Cahuenga Pass in an old history of LA, a man with a sleeping-roll slung across his back wheeling a bicycle up a long, winding dirt road, not much more than a path, toward the pass above which looked like the Borgo Pass in Transylvania to the educated eye. The picture was taken before the highway system was built, but came after the ownership of the south-land by Mexicans, whose property boundaries were distinctly laid out on the flyleaf of my history book, a misleading map which made the entire LA Basin look about the size of a K-Mart parking lot.

I drove over the pass and down toward The Valley, only I did not want to take the freeway all the way in, I wanted to get off and drive down along the base of the hills on the legendary Ventura Boulevard. I took the first panic exit and found myself driving directly into the Universal City Studios parking lot. The studio is connected to the highway. I don't mean an off-ramp, I mean the highway goes right up to a booth where you have to pay to get out.

"I made a mistake," I said to a nineteen-year-old black kid who was wearing a baby-blue sweater and the biggest smile I ever saw on someone who had to work to get money. "I got off the highway by mistake and I want to get back on. Can I turn around here and get out?"

"If you give me five dollars," he said.

I thought he was serious. This must have happened to him fifty times a day. I was ready to actually pay him the five bucks I was so shot with adrenaline and awestruck by the fact that Universal Studios possesses the power to make the California State Highway Commission give it a highway right up to its door, no off-ramp, a total highway.

"Go on through," he grinned.

I drove away thinking that this kid was just beginning his career, that he would be promoted from parking lot attendant to studio usher, to production assistant, to director, to producer, to mogul before he was thirty. He was sharp and very entertaining. I made a U-turn and drove toward an overpass and saw another car taking the fake off-ramp into Universal, and I wondered how much money the studio ultimately made from people who didn't know where they were going, a very American business strategy.

Ventura Boulevard was interesting. I envisioned people in the Twenties and Thirties cruising down the road thinking, This is it, autobahn, it makes you wanna holler solid! But it was a narrow road. It skirted the backside of the Hollywood Hills, greenery on both shoulders and shops and businesses all the way down into the Valley which must have thrived before the Universal City Studios highway came into being. It was old. It had a feel of history about it but was a little lame.

I had no preconceptions about the lay of the land and merely absorbed the onslaught of shopettes. Occasionally there would be a concrete underpass which might have been built by the WPA, but I could see that Studio City, Sherman Oaks, Encino, Tarzana, Canoga Park, Tokyo and Sri Lanka were just one long mall with Dairy Queens tucked in here and there. I turned north on Sepulveda and succumbed to that odd rapture I had felt the first night I was in town. No matter how far or how long I drove I could not get lost, and mesmerized by this notion I began turning randomly onto side streets and touring the neighborhoods, some of which were circled on my map as potential rental spots and some now crossed out. I peered at houses and tried to think who would be living here, who there, ranch-style houses, ankle-high fences bordering lawns going to pot. Technicians who worked at Universal? And did stars live here? It all looked like what had been the better homes of West Denver in the late Fifties and early Sixties, Ricky Ricardo suburban, losing its gleam. I loved it. The air was balmy and I rode with my window down and felt like I was driving through a toy town where relatives and friends who shared my interests lived, and would welcome me if I knocked on their doors.

I drove aimlessly, gripped by the spell of the San Fernando Valley surrounded by those U-shaped hills, the Simi Hills to the west, the Santa Susanna Mountains to the north, the Santa Monica and Hollywood Hills to the south, the Valley itself like a John Steinbeck alfalfa ranch, long and flat with perspectives colliding, you could see the curve of the earth in its span. I envisioned orange groves, lettuce fields, and irrigation ditches aplenty until "the movies" come and swallered up the good land, and all the noble farmers were replaced by irritable folks who stand in cranky 7-Eleven lines buying Rolaids.

I headed south noting that most of the houses were old, weatherbeaten, a lot of post-WWII clapboard. I passed through the grassy and uninhabited Sepulveda Flood Control Basin, there's a weird place, and came out unexpectedly in Encino. The road was crowded, and I felt guilty if I didn't turn left against a red light like everyone else was doing, but I wasn't going to let these maniacs intimidate me. I would teach them a lesson. I was polite at red lights and made a pest of myself, wondering how it could be that motorists who showed such fanatical respect for the rights of pedestrians could otherwise drive with such demonic contempt for the rules of the road. Could the people of Los Angeles County be so desperate to ingratiate themselves with The Beautiful People that they would put their lives on the line at intersections out of fear of being called "square?" I pondered this mystery as I cruised the sandblasted redbrick shopettes of Encino, looking for a 7-Eleven.

The sidewalks were filled with Babettes and Gogis. Casting would be a snap. I parked and went in and bought a Coke, Hostess Cupcakes, and a pack of cigarettes and went out to the car. I sat with the door open, my shoes on the warm asphalt, and looked at my map and compared it to a list of addresses of houses and apartment buildings I had culled from the morning's *LA Times*. I just wanted to see what they looked like. What did an eight hundred dollar a month house in California look like compared to one in Denver?

Girls walked along the sidewalk that ran the length of the shopette, girls in shorts. Girls in shorts. We would need only girls who could fake a fake French accent. But they would have to be dedicated girls, girls who would commit themselves to years of Babette and Gogi roles even as the wrinkles began sprouting at the corners of their eyes. Or maybe we would do it like Menudo and every year there would be a new Babette and a new Gogi, like all the *Dr. Who* characters. Twenty years from now men in their late thirties would say, "My favorite Babette was Peggy Brisnehan, the blonde one who was caught in the giant clam in the Grand Cayman episode." And his friends would say, "Fergit it, no contest, the best Babette was Kitty Lawlor," and everyone in the bar would say, "Yeah, Kitty Lawlor," and then the Peggy fan would say, "But she couldn't act worth a damn," and the others would say, "That's what made her so fun to watch," and so on, but there wouldn't be any big fights because all the guys and even their girlfriends, who used to lay on their beds at night in Des Moines and fantasize about going to Hollywood and auditioning for one of the Babette or Gogi roles, would get misty-eyed remembering what it was like to be young and ignorant of the awfulness of life and the broken hearts to come that always bypassed Babette and Gogi, who never aged, who at the end of every film sped into the sunset on the hood of a motorboat, laughing without a care and scissoring their gorgeous legs at the boys on shore.

I left Encino heading north and then east, and drove through a neighborhood made of clapboard houses that resembled the northern suburbs of Denver, with a lot of cars up on blocks in the backyards. The lawns were yellow and I wondered if grass had seasons even if Southern California itself didn't. I could envision renting one of these houses for a few months until I got established, but I could also envision just remaining in Denver until I got established and avoiding altogether the process of moving into one of these joints. But seeing these low-budget houses helped to begin to resolve a question that had been haunting me ever since I had arrived in this place which cost so much to live in, the question being, how can anyone afford to live in LA? Where do all the shopkeepers, parking-lot attendants, waitresses and car hops and secretaries and delivery boys and gas-station attendants live? I imagined thousands of workers commuting into LA from Arizona every morning. Housing prices were through the ceiling, so how could anyone afford to live in LA earning five bucks an hour? Well, they probably lived in these houses.

Of course, what I was really asking was, how could I afford to live in LA? I didn't have a movie deal yet. And if I came out here without a done deal, did I really think I was going to be doing anything different than I was doing back in Denver, which was nothing?

It had been cloudy all afternoon. I decided to go back to LA on the Golden State Freeway rather than over one of the canyon roads of the Hollywood Hills. I headed east until I hit 5 and then got onto the Hollywood Freeway headed south. Rain began falling in a steady drizzle and I instantly noticed how unbelievably fast everyone was driving in spite of the rain, and when you are going with the flow of highway traffic you can't just ease off the gas pedal and let the maniacs pass you because it's endless, you are in a river of steel. I was thinking something along this line when I saw a semi-tractor trailer ahead of me starting to swerve. The evening light was already bad because of the low clouds, and suddenly all I could see in front of me were taillights flashing like neon popcorn. Traffic far ahead had slowed and the semi driver had hit his brakes, and I watched with perverse fascination as the eighteen-wheeler began doing a hula that had disaster written all over it.

The highway was slick with fresh rain, and it was by the grace of God that there were no cars on either side of the truck. It swerved from one lane and back into the other, the desperate truck driver tapping his brakes and guiding the bastard like a surfboard, and then miraculously the cars in front of it started accelerating and everything began flowing properly and the truck and the traffic were all moving down the highway as one, but I didn't see much of that because I turned off at the next down-ramp and found myself back in Encino, sweating like a pig.

I turned at a busy intersection off Ventura and drove up the backside of the Hollywood Hills where I supposed the wealthier people lived. There were no straight streets here, no right angles, the roads rose and curved past big houses nestled against the hillsides surrounded by thick foliage, and it had a soothing effect upon me. I began wending in an easterly direction, preferring to take the longer but quieter route back toward the inevitable Golden State Freeway. The roads moved up the sides of the hills in steps, and I followed what seemed to be the main asphalt but then I turned off here and there down intriguing streets, peering at houses and remembering that no matter how far or how long I drove I could never get lost, because Ventura Boulevard was at my left, down below, except now it seemed to me that in fact it must be on my right after I took a particularly long curve past one gigantic house where all the cars parked on both sides of the road were facing the same direction even though it was not a one-way street. I stopped at an intersection and decided to drive downhill until I came again to Ventura. It was dark, somehow night had come in all this wandering. I was not bothered but wanted to get back over the hills and down into LA. A thin rain had begun falling, and I was getting hungry.

I snaked down a little asphalt street toward the hum of traffic and when I came to the main street I actually blanched and instinctively put my foot on the brake. I had been driving for what I had estimated to be twenty minutes through what I believed to be the hills of Sherman Oaks, but I found myself at a stoplight at an intersection I recognized from earlier in the day, in the very heart of Encino. A car behind me began honking and I turned right quickly and moved into the flow of traffic on Ventura Boulevard headed east, in a state of mild shock. Somehow I had gotten turned around. I had been guided inexorably back to Encino. Sure. The first time is deliberate, the second time coincidence, but the third time? How do you explain that? What rambling existential polemic might some college professor pluck from his bag of abstractions to explain my inability to get away from Encino while a light rain is falling and the sky is turning black and shifting wet white headlights are blinding me?

I was tired. In an earlier era I might have been labeled cranky. I decided, instead of searching for the Golden State Freeway, to take the first right turn and arc over the Hollywood Hills through one of the canyon roads, which in this case turned out to be Coldwater Canyon.

No matter how far you go or how long you drive, you cannot get lost in LA, I kept mumbling, watching the damn drivers forming a parade of lights behind me as I threaded my way slowly up the black wet twisted road.

By the time I reached the summit there was a line of headlights behind me backed up all the way to Sherman Oaks, impatient drivers anxious to pass me and get on down into LA so they can postpone appointments. It was raining hard now, and as I began the descent through Beverly Hills cars began to pass me, racing down the now wide black gelatinous streets to merge with the maw of traffic flowing east and west on Sunset Boulevard. But I drove slowly, and eventually found my place in the traffic flowing toward LA proper.

It was around eight. I was back among streetlights, and the brightness separated me from my trip to the San Fernando Valley, the drive through Coldwater Canyon suddenly seeming an endless and slightly skewed dream. When I got back to the motel I was exhausted and starved. I climbed the stairs to my room and opened the door to that ice-cold clean motel smell, a smell not unlike new money. I paused a moment to look at the freshly made bed, the vacuumed carpet, the sanitary strip across the toilet seat, and the cheery new-wrapped soaps. I could have wept, but instead took off my shoes and ordered a pizza by phone.

CHAPTER 6

I had served a few months at the Presidio of San Francisco when I was in the army, but had never really gone down and looked around and gotten to know the city very well, so that during my visit to Mike in 1976 it was as though I was visiting the city for the first time in my life. In the army it had always seemed like I was viewing the city through a pane of glass, in that I could never really become a part of it because I had to go back to the army base sooner or later. It made the experience not quite real. When I did go downtown I often felt like I was only pretending to visit the city. I spoke with Mike on the phone one week after he first moved out there, when both of us were swollen with the excitement of his, a member of our family, getting away from Denver and doing something with his life besides yakking endlessly about it. "I saw Francis Ford Coppola going into the St. Francis hotel," he said, and this excited me. My brother was right where it was all happening, Frisco, the happening city where the beats once roamed the streets.

On Sunday night I talked my brother into going out on the town. I had always assumed that Mike's lifestyle had changed when he moved to San Francisco. This assumption, like all the assumptions I have ever embraced in my life, was based on absolutely nothing. I discovered that his Saturday nights in San Francisco were no different than had been his, and my, Saturday nights in Denver, which consisted mostly of sitting around our basement apartment drinking beer and watching TV and reading magazines which we both subscribed to.

"Let's go out drinking," I said.

He wasn't very enthusiastic. Take away its history and glamour and ambiance and architectural wonders and San Francisco is just another city, yawn, okay, he decided it might be fun since he hadn't been out on a Saturday night in about five years.

We started in a bar just south of Golden Gate Park not far from his apartment where he told me bikers who had been in Roger Corman films used to drink. We sat in a booth and didn't talk for awhile. He was still thinking about his business. I mentioned the first time we went to see Duck's Breath Mystery Theatre. After four drinks he started reminiscing about them and I was able to put my brain in neutral and concentrate on drinking.

"Do you remember the first time you came here, and we sat on that outdoor patio at that bar on Columbus Avenue and cracked jokes about all the people who passed by?" he said.

Yes. I remembered. And I knew now that it was only one block up from City Lights bookstore and the people we were laughing at were down-and-outers, North Beach bums, the last hippies, sons of beatniks.

"That was a great night," he said.

I asked him if he remembered the day a milk truck drove into a ditch near our house in Kansas where we had lived as children. There were broken milk bottles all over the place.

"No," he said.

Nevertheless, I thought it appropriate that two brothers should reminisce about their seedy childhood. There needed to be a summing up. How did we get here? Were we really anywhere?

"Let's go there," Mike said.

"Go where?"

"To that bar on Columbus Avenue."

I didn't want to go there. I wanted to either stay here or go to a bar we had never been to before, in a part of town we had never explored. "Why don't we just drink here?" I said.

"Come on," Mike said. "Let's go to that bar."

"I'm happy right here," I said.

"Come on," he said. "Live a little."

Columbus Avenue is a circus at night, but I have to admire the parking habits of San Franciscans. If you can somehow fit your car at the gutter, or in the middle of the sidewalk, or up on someone's porch, well, that's all right. And if you happen to put a dent in the car you're trying to park behind, well, that's all right too. This city was made for pedestrians anyway. Park it anyplace you can, buddy. We're not formal around here.

A tourist was vacating a parking spot on a twisted little street northeast of Columbus Avenue, and my experienced brother quickly slipped his car into the empty space.

We got out and walked down the asphalt road to Columbus with our hands in our pockets. A slow wind was blowing and we wore our collars up like hoods and drifted past topless joints where barkers looked you right in the eye spouting their spiel. A man stumbled out of a joint furious. "They charged me eight dollars for five goddamn ounces of beer!" he shouted.

We went up the hill and stopped in front of the bar he wanted to go to, a fenced-off front patio where tourists were packed at tabletops the size of hubcaps. Standing-room only.

Waiting time for drinks: twenty-five minutes. I looked at Mike, who up until now possessed a kind of finger-popping enthusiasm for this venture. He looked at me. We went back to our car in unspoken agreement, and ultimately finished the night in a topless bar with no cover.

On Thursday morning I called Steve's office. He was editing so I left a message on his machine saying only hello. I dressed and left the hotel, and headed for the beach, away from the city that is everywhere. The color of the road and the shops was the color of the misted sky, everything gray and tan. I stopped at a McDonald's even though I told myself it was wrong to not eat at a one-of-a-kind place, but the romance of the foreign city was withering. I drove to a 7-Eleven and bought a pack of cigarettes and headed for Santa Monica and the comic-book stores.

My friend who accused me of stealing or losing his anthology of underground comics had told me to look for it if I ever got to a real city, and I spoke through my hat telling him I knew it could be found in LA even though it had been out of print a decade and was more likely to be found in San Francisco where they print the hideous things.

I had once visited Rip Off Press in San Francisco, just to see it, a big white one-story warehouse operation. I was pleased to find it in a sleazy, industrial part of town, you had to look for it and drive empty back-streets. I walked around the side and found that all the dumpsters had locks on them to keep thieves like me from stealing original artwork or sketches or what might pass for story ideas. I didn't blame them, and felt complimented in a way. I walked around a muddy field behind the warehouse looking for treasures. I was a kid once, I hadn't forgotten that treasures are found in weed fields. I came across a shoebox filled with envelopes. I stooped in the mud and looked at them, pre-printed return mailing addresses of the People's Temple. I smirked with pleasure, odd, the Jim Jones massacre was old news. I got up and walked away from the box without even taking one single envelope as a souvenir. When I got back to Denver my friend was incensed that I could not at least have brought back one of these collector's items, and it was only at that moment, in the bar, with him hounding me, that I realized I had suffered a lapse of cultural protocol. How could it be that in the very throes of weed-field souvenir hunting I did not think to take even one People's Temple envelope with me?

The comic-book store was on Santa Monica Boulevard in a good-looking storefront. Everything was nice, like City Lights bookstore. The fire in the belly that motivated bohemians or poets to start underground comics and publishing companies inevitably led them to sensible business practices and picayune cost accounting. That was okay, though. Everything was okay because everything was a lesson, a humiliating growth-oriented lesson. In high school they told us You Have Got To Be Mature.

I wandered the aisles, it was a large place, the walls stocked with the latest underground comics. Mostly young people, but there were middle-class mothers and their rebel sons purchasing the kiddy underground comics, and pimply teenagers in leather eyeballing ink tits. I found the adult section and looked in vain and knew all along the anthology would not be there, that I would return to Denver skunked.

I asked a clerk if they had the book and he giggled and apologized and said I would have to ask Bill. Bill was a kid with long hair, real long hair, he had a kind of New York grayness about him, and wore a ratty trench-coat. I thought he must be the owner of the store because he was sitting by the cash register fiddling with paperwork and looking unhappy.

"Bill, do we have *The Apex Treasury of Underground Comics?*" the clerk said.

Bill peered at the clerk, and then at me. "No," he said. "That's been out of print a long time." He put down his paperwork and looked at the ceiling. "That's a great collection. It has a drawing by R. Crumb on the cover, a street scene, a close-up of a comic lying in the gutter and a foot walking past." He sat there and described the book like some kind of underground art historian. Then he stood up. "Let me go take a look in the back room."

He was gone about five minutes. I stared at comics in a glass display case feeling like a chump. Everyone in the store had heard our conversation.

Bill came walking back out of the stockroom carrying a copy. Twenty bucks. I was in a big city.

When I got to Venice Beach I was buoyed once again by that mesmerizing spell that had engulfed me the day I arrived in the show biz capital of the world. I locked my comic in the trunk and walked up to the roller-skate sidewalk and watched the street performers with their cardboard collection boxes, playing guitars and singing on the sandy sidewalk. The weight-lifting pit. Muscle Beach where Steve Reeves once balanced women on his raised palms, but they don't call it that anymore. I had seen a color photo of the heyday, just after World War II. Same buildings, same sand, where are all the musclemen?

The guy who juggles chainsaws was there, making the nervous crowd gasp, laugh, smatter applause. "Those cardboard boxes are for donations!" All up and down the beach people who didn't want real jobs sweating under a foggy sun for bucks. What could I do to make people put dollars in a box? I asked myself. I could sit at a card table on the sidewalk typing stories. I could do what a few of the kids were doing, playing the blues-harp badly, bad amateur mime, panhandling. I could panhandle maybe. Even that, you probably would have to get good at.

I went down to the beach, which was deserted, the long noisy gray waves sweeping in, leaving shiny bulbous seaweed. I looked for shells. I found a few. Blue, purple, the color of royalty churned from the ocean's belly. The water was freezing. I stood on the beach and looked north and south, way up to Malibu, and way down to where Palos Verdes disappeared in the mist. It probably had looked like this to D.W. Griffith. Had probably looked like this to the Mexican colonists. Boiling with potential, but not much happening.

CHAPTER 7

I asked my brother if he would loan me his car to drive down to Monterey. The one hard-to-get-to beat landmark was south of there, a bridge that spanned two cliffs where Ferlinghetti's cabin was supposed to be. Jack Kerouac had written about it in *Big Sur*, and before I went back to Denver I felt I ought to go and see it because I didn't think I would ever be back this way again. In LA I never did get to the La Brea Tar Pits. A friend later told me they were no big deal. But that wasn't the point.

Mike didn't want to go, he had business at his shop to take care of, but then, when I was packing some sandwiches and looking at a map and asking him a few questions about State Highway 1, he said to hell with it and told me he would go with me, which I thought was a fabulous and beat thing to do, since I was sacrificing nothing and he was saying, "Let's close the shop today and drive!" which was what I assumed Neal Cassady would have said if he had ever owned a shop.

About one mile south of Monterey something went wrong with the car. It was losing power. I was glad my brother had decided to come along because it was his car and if I had gotten stranded in Big Sur I wouldn't have thought it was cool and beat at all, I would have been horrified and disgusted. Mike popped the hood and looked it over and discovered that the gas line to the carburetor had split open. He walked across the road to a gas station and came back with a piece of rubber tubing and fixed it. "That'll hold us until we get back to San Francisco."

"Do we have to go back?" I said.

"Hell no, we can go on." He had aplomb. If he hadn't been there I probably would have caught a bus to Denver and sent him a telegram C.O.D. "Your car is in Monterey stop."

We didn't know which of the big spans was the one Kerouac described in his book, we had to guess. We drove until we came to the most likely-looking bridge, a creepy bastard that arched over a canyon which opened to the ocean. Mike parked the car at the edge of the road and we got out and looked around. I looked to the very bottom of the bridge because there supposedly were wrecks which Neal Cassady and Jack Kerouac had gone to look at one day, cars that had careened off the cliff. I couldn't see anything. I expected to see rusted brown hulks in the sun. It was a sunny day. We had left the fog in the northern peninsula.

My brother walked across the road.

"Ferlinghetti," he said. He was standing beside a row of mailboxes belonging to the people who owned cabins at the bottom of the canyon accessed by a dirt road which snaked down the hillsides.

I crossed the road and looked at the mailbox. Hand-painted letters faded badly by sunlight, you could barely read them, but there they were, the letters, the word: Ferlinghetti.

I aimed my camera and took a little picture, and for maybe four seconds I felt something. Touched the past. Then it was over.

★ ★ ★

I was brushing my teeth when the phone rang. I turned off the water and set my toothbrush down and cleared my throat. There was only one person who knew my phone number at the Farmer's Market motel.

"Mr. Palmer?"

"Yes?"

"This is Fred's agent. How are you doing?"

"Great."

"The reason I'm calling is to let you know that Fred appreciates your coming out here and he really did like your script, but we've decided to go in another direction and we won't be pursuing your film project."

It was my turn to talk. "Is that right?" My voice sounded thin to me.

"So . . . Fred wanted me to tell you he was glad to have had the opportunity to look at your ideas, and if we decide to work with you on any projects in the future we'll get in touch with you."

Good-bye.

"Well, thank you for calling me."

Good-bye.

"You're quite welcome, Mr. Palmer."

Good-bye.

"Good-bye."

Good-bye.

"Good-bye."

I tuned in on the middle of an episode of *Gunsmoke* about two years after Strother Martin died, late at night, too late even to call my friend who was a fan. It was a two-part show and both parts were broadcast back-to-back late at night on Channel 2 in Denver.

Strother Martin was playing desert scum who had fought like hell for the Big Break. He was a gold miner out in the desert, and had been stranded in a kind of rocky oasis for ten years because he was too far away from civilization to walk back, and his poor mule had died long ago. He lived where there was a spring with fresh water. He had bags of gold dust that he had mined but was unable to take back to town. Then Festus Hagan showed up. Strother took Festus prisoner and forced him at gunpoint to carry gourds containing bags of gold dust dangling from a pole across his back.

Festus led Strother across the desert, and they sipped water now and then and were tense and miserable and argumentative. Strother wanted to get back to town where he believed everybody would hate him for being a rich man. His dream was to make them writhe with envy at his success. He and Festus trudged across the desert for almost the entire episode, and when they finally got to the town where everyone would remember Strother the Gold Miner, they found the town abandoned. It was a ghost town.

When the show had begun I made one phone call to my friend to announce a "Strother Alert." When no one answered after four rings I hung up and felt wracked with guilt for two reasons. I was afraid I had awakened his family, and I was afraid I had hung up too soon and he would have wanted me to wake him to see this show.

So I sat in my apartment drinking pink chablis and watched as Strother Martin began to hallucinate that people were cheering him, he could see women and men, translucent ghosts, leaning out of windows, and he waved at them, waving his bags of gold.

Meanwhile Festus dropped the pole and went looking for water, fully aware that something was wrong with his captor. Festus found an old well and drew the bucket and drank. Then he went looking for Strother.

Strother was in the cemetery. He was looking at the names of all his old enemies carved in granite on tombstones, the names of all the people he had hated and had dreamed for years of confronting with his riches and success. But they were all dead, buried six feet under, and there was no one left to sneer at, no one to whom he could lift his bags of gold and shout, "See! I did it! I'm not scum! I'm a rich man, rich enough to buy this town ten times over!"

His desert dreams were all for nothing, and that's what he began saying. He lifted a bag of gold and began belting a tombstone with it and shouting, "It was all fer nuthin! It was all fer nuthin!" and the bag broke, and the gold dust scattered among the graves.

Then he collapsed. Festus tried to help him but he was a goner. The show drew to its close with Festus holding in his arms this poor old desert rat while the wind blew all the gold dust out onto the prairie.

Marshal Dillon showed up about that time, the kind of twist an experienced screenwriter would think up for a good denouement. Everyone watching the show knew by now that despite what he had been through, in the end Festus did not hate that old man for what he had done. He understood. Even Marshal Dillon seemed to understand that something significant had happened here. Understanding is everything. Understanding can change the way a person feels about things. It no doubt says that somewhere in the Bible.

PART THREE

AUTUMN

When Palmer made the decision to go down to one of the Denver cab companies and apply for work as a driver, it was as though he had surrendered finally to his worst fear, had given up any pretense that there was any hope that he would ever find a job that both paid well and did not drain the life out of his soul from the moment he arrived in the morning until he left at night. He knew other men who drove cabs for a living, but until the night he realized he would never again be able to work at a real job he had never entertained for a moment the idea of prowling the streets of Denver in search of people who did not own cars. He had rarely ridden in a taxi as an adult, and possessed exactly one vague memory of riding in a cab when he was a child: he and his mother seated on the strange gray slick backseat of a car driven by a fat stranger in a T-shirt.

Once his decision was made, and he had asked the cab drivers he knew about the process for applying for work (clean copy of your driving record, no recent DUI), once he had gotten into his own heap of an ancient Chevy and began driving toward the northern industrial section of Denver where the cab companies were located, he felt as though he were entering a dream, the softcore nightmare of once again going to a place to ask someone for work, the same nightmare he had lived through since he had left home at eighteen, since he had gone out into the world on his own to pursue those secret ill-formed ambitions of youth, whatever they were. He had turned forty-two a few weeks earlier, and could not

believe that twenty-four years after he had left home to make
his way in the world he was making his way to a smog-riddled
warehouse district where he had once held a job as an ice-
cream delivery driver, a job which he had quit like all the
jobs he had quit throughout the years, jobs whose bosses
and foremen and supervisors had drained the life out of him
every time they opened their mouths and told him to pick
this up and carry it over there. That's what working was.
That's what unskilled labor was. Muscle. Someone else
provided the brain, the plan, but how could someone who
had read more than three thousand books during his lifetime
take orders from men whose craving for stories was satisfied
by saloons, the foremen of jobs which were as bad as he was
certain cab driving was going to be.

Part of the dreamlike quality of this journey north was the
familiar trepidation in his gut which he had first experienced
when applying for his first real job ever, a job at a furniture
store he absolutely had to have at eighteen because he had
run out of money and had no way to get food. Twenty-four
years later, on a Monday morning, he drives down a quiet
side street in Denver toward the dirty whitewashed walls of
a large one-story building surrounded by a cyclone fence in
slight disrepair, and he feels that tightening in his gut, the
fright of youth. How can this be? I served in Vietnam. I've
had a thousand shit jobs. Cab driving is the bottom rung, you
cannot go any lower than this without taking up residence in
an alley littered with wine bottles. What was this juvenile fear
that some man behind a desk will shake his head and hand
your driving record back to you and say, "Sorry." Palmer has
seen the sorts of men who drive cabs. How could they have

made it through this looming obstacle course, these men who speak bad English and never seem to bathe?

That was part of the dreamlike experience, which was more intense than usual, now that he needed the job, his mind manufacturing a monologue of self-righteous outrage as he parked his heap at a curb and shut off the engine and pulled his driving record out of his shirt pocket and looked at it again. No recent DUI. Clean record. This was the single scrap of pride that he could call his own at the age of forty-two: a blank sheet of paper.

He looked at his face in the rear-view mirror and brushed flat his short-cropped beard that had turned white with an amazing quickness the year he turned forty. He got out of the car and was pleased to note that the little barking bitch of apprehension did not slow him down or give him second thoughts. Three times he had walked past the upholstery shop where he had gotten his first job before he got up the nerve to go in and apply. Sofa beds to be lifted onto a truck and delivered to the homes of customers. The owner hired him on the spot, which surprised Palmer. Too easy. His fears had laughed at him then, ridiculed him.

The unnatural crimp of good shoes, his Sunday shoes that he had worn only to weddings and funerals, the thin soles scuffing the sidewalk, added to the lilt of unreality on this quest for an income. Tennis shoes were all that he ever wore nowadays, forty-two years old and still dressing like a kid. Still wore blue jeans, but for today he had pulled out an old pair of Levi corduroys with the nap still intact, a good-looking dark blue pair of pants which Miller Stockman had stopped stocking two year earlier. Black shoes polished for church, and good dark blue pants to impress the personnel clerk whom, he had been told, he would have to speak to.

As he walked toward the single door in the strangely windowless wall of the building, the mid-afternoon sun bouncing off the white paint and splashing him with the last of the summer heat made his eyes water. End of September, when everything begins to die but which to anyone who has ever gone to school is rife with the promise of new beginnings, resolutions, ambitions that are no longer accompanied by the odor of burning fallen leaves. City ordinance. Clean air is more important than poetry. As he turned the brass knob, pushed the door inward, and saw in the bright fluorescent lighting the green-painted walls and simple bleak furnishings of the taxi office headquarters, he felt as though he were back in the army.

"May I help you?"

The room contained a large metal table scattered with papers, two chairs, a space where cabbies would sit at the table to fill out official forms but would not hang around to smoke or shoot the shit. A black woman was looking at him through a doorway to an adjoining room, leaning off to the side of her desk to see him. Very military to him, a clumsy make-do situation, the receptionist has to lean to look through a doorway, almost unprofessional but it works. This is, after all, only a cab company.

"I'd like to apply to be a driver," he said.

"Do you have a copy of your current driving record?"

He reached into his shirt pocket and produced the paperwork, handed it to her feeling rather good about his competence. I bathe regularly, speak good English, and have the proper paperwork. I will be hired for these three reasons alone.

"Clean as a whistle," she said, lifting her eyes from the paper and smiling at him. How often did she get to say this? Her hair was done up, she was wearing lipstick, golden rings on her arms and fingers. Sitting very erect in a burgundy-colored dress with white flowers, and sporting red-rimmed glasses with large round lenses, big red girl-glasses which she removed and set on her desk as she opened a drawer and pulled out the paperwork prepared for men like Palmer who walk in off the street between the hours of 8 a.m. and 5 p.m. Application form, personal history, fill in the blanks, social security number, etc., as well as a two-page test which he was required by the city to take.

"Just have a seat at that table," the woman said, pointing toward the foyer. "When you've finished filling out everything including the test, bring it back to me."

Very much like the army, especially now that a different door in the foyer opened just as he was sitting down, with three men entering talking noisily, like officers or NCOs, obviously employees. A noisy and busy place. Palmer ignored them, set to work with the pen that he had made a special point of bringing with him. A college habit, an annoyed professor once saying, "I thought all students carried pens at all times." Palmer had thought at the time, This is a thing that distinguishes scholars from the rest of the world, they always have access to a pen in the way that addicts always have access to a drug.

He glanced at the test before filling out the application. City landmarks, locations of destinations, businesses, service

centers where he would most likely be dropping off customers.
Stapleton Airport. Union Station. Currigan Hall. Elitch's.
There were thirty dots on a crudely hand-drawn city map,
and he had to match the dots with the place-names typed on
a separate sheet. Simpleminded, but then he ended up having
trouble with the five dots located in midtown, and after his
test was graded he was told that he had incorrectly identified
the main bus terminal as the Hilton Hotel.

Annoyed at first by the thought that his mistake might
have cost him the job, he later was annoyed at missing a
question so simpleminded. The woman reviewed his application, told him everything looked good, and that all he had
to do was make an appointment for a physical. If he passes
his physical, he has to bring the paperwork back here, then
she will send him downtown to take another test at the Civic
Center for his cab license, and he'll be in business.

A series of steps, a pain in the ass which having been
completed will give him a sense of satisfaction, as had his
fifteen minutes at the license bureau at Sixth and Bannock,
where he had gone at 8 a.m. to be first in line to get his driving
record. He was in fact ninth in line, but when he was handed
his record and saw the blank box where infractions were
typed, an empty box, it had made him smile. He had tucked
it into his pocket and walked out into the autumn morning
and breathed deeply the leafless smog. I am unblemished. I
will skate through this process and by Friday customers at
their drop-off points will be handing me cash, and that knot
in my gut will begin to loosen. Next month's rent will be paid.
Cold cash is like a weapon that keeps the world at bay.

He drove away from the cab company flush with the
feeling of having not failed, and decided to drive past the

clinic where he would be taking his physical, to make certain
of its location. It was a few miles east of the cab company, a
functional bunker where MDs certified men to drive cabs,
trucks, busses, any motorized vehicle which might endanger
the public safety should the driver be unfit to guide a ton or
more of steel. Sudden heart attack. Blood infested with illegal
drugs, or even legal. Eyes too weak to read the messages
posted along the thoroughfares, speed limit 55, no passing,
no exit, slow, yield, wrong way, stop.

He was a bit worried about the last item. He had never
worn glasses in his life, but knew his eyesight was getting
bad, things in the distance were blurred, but he was so used
to dealing with indiscernible approaching objects which
suddenly snapped into familiarity at the last moment that it
never bothered him. He had passed every eye test at every
motor vehicle department he had ever gone to since he was
sixteen.

The clinic was surrounded by cars, a few trucks, one large
semi lurking behind the building where the cyclone fence ran
along Interstate 70. He would be up at 7 a.m. and arrive here
at 8 a.m. to beat the crowd. This was his decision. No more
Coca-Cola for the rest of the day. A friend who drove for
Yellow Cab had told him the secret of the piss test: drink
nothing but water for 24 hours prior to going for your physical
and you'll pee clean enough to wash a windshield.

Palmer had not undergone a physical since he had gotten
out of the army. Almost the last step before they handed him
his discharge. He stood in front of an X-ray machine with his
arms raised over his head, and decided that they would find
cancer in his lungs. Smoke your way through a year in Vietnam,
then come to the kind of justice you are used to. He could

always feel death hanging around down the block of his life. But no, no cancer, they let him go with a smile and a promise that if he wanted to reenlist they would be more than happy to have him back. All the giddy privates and corporals climbing onto a bus for their ride out of Fort Lewis. A drill sergeant walked by the bus and everybody hollered at him. He waved at the veterans. Everybody rode the bus to Sea-Tac airport believing that they were about to get on with their lives.

On the way back to his apartment Palmer stopped off at a Salvation Army store to pick up a pair of dumbbells which on a previous trip he had seen resting on the concrete floor in a corner among a clutter of unwanted athletic equipment. The knowledge that he soon would be lifting suitcases into the trunk of a cab at the airport put him in mind of just how out of shape he was. Not since he had delivered sofa beds as a teenager had he done any strenuous physical labor. Delivering ice cream to restaurants and grocery stores had involved a fair amount of lifting, but he'd had a dolly to bear those frozen burdens. He had fooled around with barbells in the army and later in college, but that was another lifetime, that was before serious relationships with women, that was when dreams quickened daily and everything beyond the horizon was a promising mystery. One of the women he'd lived with had given away his 110-pound barbell set in one of those woman flurries that all the females he'd known were consumed by toward the end of each relationship. Clean everything out, throw away the old, make room for the new, see that the closet floor is spotless. He was the last useless item she had thrown out.

The Salvation Army store had once been a Safeway. The shell and familiar Quonset arc of the roof still remained, but the inside had been hollowed out. The ancient linoleum floors bore the scars where the cashier counters had stood, conveyor belts hauling food, rapid fingers of middle-aged women stabbing numbered buttons which made a crashing sound ringing up totes. Wonder Bread 35¢ a loaf in his youth. Now there was only one cash register on a glass-walled counter inside of which lay selected items deemed too valuable by the manager of the store to be left out on the shelves. Jewelry mostly, watches and rings, a few toys that might be worth something to a collector. A young black woman, perhaps nineteen, stood at the counter with her hands clasped, staring out the window at the passing traffic.

Palmer made his way through the clothing racks where elderly women fingered sweaters and dresses, clutched black purses to their bosoms, and glanced at him with the querulous eyes of his dead mother. He began to worry. The dumbbells would not be there, two sleek-looking black bars with hexagonal bells which would help out in his new job, tone his arms, prevent sudden rupture, thwart failure in its per-petual stalking tracks. He hurried past the paperback shelves—the only reason he ever came into this store was to look at old paperbacks and collect the collectibles. Readers discarded amazing things. First editions, Faulkners, beat literature, a mint condition Catcher in the Rye which he had copped for a quarter, hurrying out of the store like an ecstatic thief.

The dumbbells were there, with dust one layer thicker on their flat edges than the last time he'd seen them, buried beneath a slovenly rack of skis. No bodybuilders looking for bargains. He had to do a bit of digging, stepping over a rowing machine, standing awkwardly with his legs spread as he grappled with one and then the other of the weights, understanding that this was where he would rupture himself if it was ever going to happen. Every decision I ever made was wrong, he told himself, as he had begun telling himself at some point during the past ten years, but also knowing that this truth was useless. Each iron item bore a small green sticker, a price tag. Two dollars per. He loved these stores, loved flea markets, loved free enterprise in its least-regulated form.

He carried his swag like suitcases to the counter and hoisted them to show to the black woman, then set them on the floor rather than on the glass countertop.

The woman reached toward the cash register, then glanced at Palmer's white beard and said, "Sir . . . do you qualify for the Senior Citizen's Discount?"

The first job Palmer ever had that he knew was not going to last involved delivering flowers. It paid only a dollar a delivery, but he loved the job. People were always happy to see him, always smiled when they opened the door, flowers for me? But he realized it would end sooner than he expected on the day he was sent to a mortuary to deliver a floral arrangement. He was told by his boss that he would have to pass through a room filled with recently deceased people in order to get to the office where the flowers would be dropped off. He would be making a delivery to the place at least once a week. He was so demoralized by the prospect that when he arrived at the funeral home he couldn't bring himself to go in the back door. He went in the front door and pretended that he didn't understand the procedure. The mortician seemed irritated, and explained it to him. When he walked out of the mortuary he knew he would keep the job only a few weeks, long enough to give him enough money to start looking for another job.

The second job he held that he knew was not going to last consisted of delivering cardboard buckets of ice cream to restaurants and small grocery stores. He did not get along with the other drivers, and was old enough to realize that you not only can't stay with a job you hate, you don't even have to, because the world is filled with terrible jobs. His job delivering furniture ended when he was drafted into the army. While in college he took summer jobs that ended in autumn, the time of death and new beginnings. One summer he was an assistant maintenance man at a plastics factory, working under the supervision of an alcoholic handyman whose frail, skinny frame seemed incapable of bearing the weight of the tool belt that he strapped on every morning with trembling hands.

After Palmer had gotten out of high school he took all the shit jobs that he knew he would have to take, knowing that none of them would last because he knew he was going to get drafted. He felt suspended in time, felt that he was only marking time, doing shit work that he didn't care about and not caring if he did his job well. He was just waiting for his draft notice. And after he went into the army he had felt the same way, suspended in time and not caring, and waiting only for his discharge. But he had thought those feelings would come to an end once he was out of the army and was free for the rest of his life, only to go on to college and find himself bored and waiting for college to end so he could again get on with his life. And after college it was all shit jobs again because there was nothing that he wanted to do for a living, did not want to get up every day and go to work for the same company for forty years as his father had done, and all the fathers of his friends, going to work every day, all of them veterans of World War II, married, families, even at fifteen he had wondered if there wasn't more to life than just that. Grow up, get married, have kids, die. Everybody was doing it.

When he got home from the Salvation Army store he looked at his face in the bathroom mirror, looked at his white beard that apparently was a signal of old age. He wondered if the cab job would last. He wanted it to last years, which the good jobs never did, wanted to make enough money from it to pay the landlord, the grocer, the gods, to give him the breathing room which in the past had seemed supplied by nothing more than youth itself.

He thought about shaving off his beard. He'd begun growing it in college when the follicles were still a dark brown, when his inherent laziness manifested itself. He had grown it because he was done with the army, and did not have to work because his education, room, and board were all being paid for by the GI Bill. He'd had to shave daily in the army, and had gotten tired of it. Was tired even of brushing his teeth, and thought about inventing some sort of device the size of an egg which a person could lather with toothpaste and then bite down on, minuscule brushes revolving inside the mouth cleaning the teeth. The chore would be over in five seconds. And he would just as soon be a nudist as cart his dirty clothes to the nearest laundromat once a week.

He decided not to shave. He spent a half-hour toying with the dumbbells, doing curls, a few overhead presses, and wondering whether to go to a flea market and buy a whole outfit, a cheap bench and barbells and really do this up right. But how could a man too lazy to shave expect to make any progress lifting weights? He drank glasses of water that evening, read part of a book, and kept glancing at the clock. At eleven he was not tired, but he went to bed and set the alarm for 7 a.m. For breakfast he intended to drink three glasses of water so that when the doc got around to asking him for a urine sample, he would open a floodgate.

He arrived at the clinic at five minutes to eight on Tuesday morning and was surprised by all the cars and trucks that had gotten there ahead of him, and he realized that a physical checkup would be an annual chore to most of these men, the lifer cabbies who already held their numbers in their hands and waited to be called to the labyrinthian back rooms where tattooed truckers with continents under their belts stood naked and judged by doctors in long clean white frocks.

A small woman, a nurse, seemed to be in charge of things in the waiting area, hurrying around with a clipboard in her hands, telling the men in jean jackets and engineer boots to go here and there. She was old, hair in a bun, was brisk, and had a grating voice, Ruth Gordon with hair tinted red. Palmer took a number from the dispensing machine at the front counter where clerks were silently processing paperwork and fees. Twenty-five dollars for a department of transportation physical. How many hundreds of drivers came through here each day, each week, each year? Doctors getting rich off the law.

Palmer was an old hand at waiting, had first learned to wait well in the army, and had taken the lessons with him. He sat on a vinyl-upholstered chair in the lobby and pulled a paperback book out of his jacket pocket. He barely got a page read before his name was called. He got up and was led to the rear of the building by Nurse Gordon. First order of business: urine. She handed him a small paper cup and pointed at a door and told him to give her a specimen.

The door opened on a closet of a toilet right off the hallway, and when he closed the door he could hear people walking back and forth, could hear the nurse breathing right outside the door, waiting for him to get on with it. A quick shot and the cup was full, then he had to spend a minute emptying the remainder of his bladder.

He left the closet and set the cup on a tray, and the nurse took it away for processing. She returned and led him to the eye test. Palmer bent his head toward a pair of binoculars, gazed at a yellow-backed screen covered with alphanumeric symbols, and failed to read the second line from the bottom even though the nurse gave him three chances. He squinted, flexed his eyeballs, reshaped those gelatinous bulbs, made uneducated guesses at the letters or numbers, he couldn't tell, and when he stood up from the machine the woman gave him a concerned look.

"You need glasses," she said.

Every decision I ever made was wrong, Palmer thought. This is not going to work. This job is not going to last. It probably won't even begin.

"Well . . . follow me," the nurse said, and Palmer obeyed, his eyes fixed on the slope of her shoulders as she led him down the hall toward an examination room.

"Take off all your clothes and put this on," she said, pointing at a white paper dressing gown lying folded on the examination table.

It will take forever to get a pair of glasses, Palmer told himself as he began to strip. What do glasses cost? Too much for a man who has no money. He hung his jeans and shirt on a chrome-plated clothes rack, stuffed his underwear down his jeans, stood naked for the time it took to unfold the dressing gown, to figure out the front from the back, put it on feeling like a kid in a school play. The doctor will now look at your dick. Women make lunch conversations about gynecologists, talk about their vaginas like garage mechanics discussing carburetors. A man without pants hasn't got a chance.

The doctor is tall, slightly balding, has a mustache, a reassuring bedside manner that Palmer is certain you'd need if your job was to tell hundreds of men a day to show you their dicks. The doc is clutching a clipboard, has a benign smile on his face. "Your urine sample was outstanding," he says. "Whatever it is you do, keep on doing it."

But Palmer will be going back to drinking twelve Cokes a day as soon as he is certified. The doctor asks questions about previous medical history, any problems? Drug addiction? Alcoholism? Heart disease? No, Palmer lies. All I want to do is drive a cab and fade into the woodwork of the world. "Do you smoke?"

Palmer lies again, says no, but he smokes when he goes to parties or plays poker, and knows that he will smoke driving a cab. But he doesn't want this written down on an official document. Nobody's business. Make people stop watching TV first. Make people stop jogging. Take away cake and ice cream, haute cuisine and model trains, take away movies and boats and vegetables, make everybody give up everything that prevents their lives from becoming unbearable.

"Lift it," the doctor says. Palmer tugs the hem of his paper skirt. The doctor examines his dick from four feet away, doesn't step close to feel around, make him cough. "Ever had any problems?"

"No," Palmer replies. "I lift weights."

After the doctor leaves, Palmer gets dressed, thinking about the doctor's job. Is this what the man had aspired to when he went to medical school? Doesn't every doctor want to start a private practice, join a clinic, get rich? But then maybe this doctor is making money hand-over-fist. You never can tell. Giving physicals to drivers might be like discovering oil. You don't have to create oil, you just suck it out of the earth and sell it. What a racket.

He finishes dressing, ties his tennis shoes, and walks down the hallway into the lobby where the nurse explains what has to be done.

"As soon as you get your glasses, come back and we'll give you the eye test again. You'll pass, and then you'll be certified."

Palmer thanks her, leaves the building, gets into his car and leans back against woven fabric made hot by the rising sun, and sighs. Nothing can be easy, everything has to be hard. He drives to the cab company thinking that it will take days to get a new pair of glasses. There was a time when a minor obstacle like this would cause him to say to hell with it and find something else to do. But this job was his last option. He will have to tell the taxi secretary that he needs to go to an optometrist, that he won't be able to continue processing until this is taken care of. Got through the army without glasses, got through life in a blur, but maybe things were clearer when he was young. Forty-two years old and driving a heap to a cab company to tell a woman he needs new glasses. It makes him want to go home and forget it, but he can't. Alleys and wine and a slow and merciless death putting the cap on a slow and merciless life.

"Are you nearsighted or farsighted?" the secretary said.

"I don't know," he replied. "I've never worn glasses before."

The secretary rolled her chair back from her desk and whipped off her big red girl-glasses and handed them to Palmer. "Try these on."

Palmer took the glasses and slipped them on and the world changed before his eyes. The far wall of the office had a wooden texture and was not simply a brown-painted wall.

And he could see individual strands of the woman's hair, molded details of her earrings. It was as if he had burst through the surface of a murky pond into the transparent miracle of air.

"Can you see better?" she said.

He nodded, twisting his neck, looking around the room, at a calendar, at the lit buttons of a phone, and didn't quite know how to express his delight at this mundane miracle.

"I'll call the clinic and tell them you're coming back for another eye test," she said, and she had the receiver in her hand and was dialing before he could voice an objection. He knew instinctively that he would not get away with this.

She spoke to someone on the other end, a clinic clerk, told the person that Mr. Palmer would be right back for his eye test. Palmer considered saying, "Whoa," but realized that this was not his idea anyway. He would again be swept off to some incomprehensible fate just as in his youth he had been swept off to the army, swept into airplanes, swept to the shores of Vietnam, swept home again.

The woman hung up the phone. "They're expecting you," she said with a smile, guileless conspirator, anything goes at this cab company.

Palmer left, got into his car and sat for a moment trying the glasses on. He could clearly see the stop sign at the end of the block, which became a blur when he raised the glasses. He lowered them and each individual white letter S coated with a sparkling paint T which would glow at night O bathed in an approaching headlight P was as clear as if he were looking at a photograph. Some things in life were not bullshit, and this was one of them.

All the way to the clinic he kept raising and lowering the glasses, marveling at how soft shapes in the distance suddenly clicked into telephone poles, pedestrians, approaching cars. He looked at himself in the rear-view mirror. The big red girl-glasses looked ridiculous on him. How could anybody at the clinic possibly believe that a man, a cab driver, would wear such glasses which had looked rather good on the woman in the office. He had to think this out, so he stopped playing with his eyeballs and began mulling it over.

He parked close to the clinic door, took off his glasses and tucked them into his shirt pocket. He got out of his car and went inside, strode up to the counter and gave his name, said the cab company had sent him over. The clerk nodded, told him to have a seat, his name would be called.

He sat on a chair in the lobby, picked up a copy of *People* magazine and began flipping through the pages. Lots of photographs, the paragraphs little more than cut-lines, the publisher who had conceived this magazine knew what he was doing, people don't want to work for their news and entertainment.

"Did you get glasses?"

Palmer lowered the magazine. Nurse Gordon was standing in front of him, bright-eyed, big smile. Palmer nodded, touched his breast pocket where the specs were hidden.

"Put 'em on! Let's see 'em!" the woman sang out.

Palmer glanced around the lobby. No place to run. Busted. He reached into his pocket, pulled out the glasses and put them on.

The smile faded from the nurse's face. She gazed at him for a few hours, then said in an oddly indifferent voice, "They're nice," and walked away.

Palmer slipped the glasses back into his pocket and sat silently, futilely on the chair with the unread magazine on his lap. His name was called over the PA. He walked up to the counter. A different nurse approached and asked him to accompany her to the eye station. He did not put on the glasses until he was leaning down toward the binoculars. Then removed them just as quickly when he stood up. He passed the test and was given his medical certification papers. He left the clinic, got into his car without putting the glasses on, and drove back to the cab company whispering, "Christ, Christ, Christ."

The test at the Civic Center on Wednesday morning was simplistic, military in its way, and went quickly. Palmer received his cab license that same day, a laminated rectangle of thin cardboard, looked like the licenses you see posted inside taxis in movies, frowned at by an actor threatening to report the obnoxious cabbie to the supervisor.

Palmer went back to his apartment and made lunch, and contemplated the final step: reporting for work on his first day, going in early to see if a cab was available since he had decided not to sign up for a regular shift just yet. If this job was not going to turn out to be real, he wanted it to be as unreal as possible. Another first day on a new job, like all the jobs he had started ever since he left home, the unpleasantness of newness that made each first day a trial, not so different from being the new kid at school. The day he reported for work at the furniture reupholstery shop, his foreman had told

him to go outside and help load furniture onto a truck. First
assignment of his adult life, he went outside quickly, eager
to do a good job, to show his boss he was capable of perform-
ing the work at hand, but when he got outside there was no
truck in sight. He looked up and down the street, walked to
the corner, saw nothing. His heart sank. He returned to the
shop and told the foreman there was no truck outside.

The foreman was a lean man in his fifties, crew-cut gray
hair, would have been cast as an irritable lawyer in a comedy.
He took Palmer by the arm and led him outside and pointed
at a large truck which had only just that moment pulled up
in the parking lot. Two men were unloading chairs.

"That truck," the foreman said with disgust, releasing
Palmer's arm and walking back into the shop. This set the
tone for the six months until Palmer quit.

On Wednesday afternoon he went down to the cab
company for a two-hour driver safety class, mandatory,
you couldn't drive without it. The room was filled with men
who resembled draftees. Young men, old men, and men
Palmer's age, wearing mostly blue jeans although the older
men tended toward slacks. Beards, mustaches, hats, coats of
many colors, each man cloaked in his own world, waiting
silently for the safety supervisor to finish explaining the
rules of the road, waiting for the video of a horrendous
traffic accident to reach its instructive climax. A short test.
Any questions? No.

This was followed by a short written test that everyone
passed, and brought to a conclusion the hurdles that Palmer
and the other men had been forced to negotiate by laws
which pretended to weed out the unfit. Except who but the

unfit would be here to begin with? Nobody spoke as they left the classroom. Nobody had a friend here. Each man, like Palmer, had come to cab driving for reasons that he might not necessarily be able to articulate. Like men reenlisting in the army after a 6-year hitch. It's the only place that'll have you.

He drove home that night and worked out for fifteen minutes with the dumbbells. He performed curls, then held them straight down at his sides and raised his shoulders as though he were hefting suitcases and getting ready to fling them into the trunk of a cab. He regretted now that he had not continued the workouts he had started in college, before beer and whiskey and cigarettes and loafing and despair had sapped the tone from his muscles. He'd been on an intramural volleyball team in college, had run with friends who took part in marathons, though he himself didn't, had run only for the pleasure of it. He had learned to love running in the army, in basic training, which he had gone through twenty-three years earlier, and could not believe it had been so long because he felt like the same person now as he had been then. How can this be? How can it have been so many years? I still listen to rock 'n' roll, movies still excite me, I wear blue jeans. After fifteen minutes his biceps began to ache and he set the dumbbells on the floor and sat in a chair and watched a weather report on TV.

He had never cared about weather reports before, since weather had meant nothing to him at any time in his life. He had never even put his head out an open window to examine the sky, but now the weather reports at ten-fifteen every night would be followed as closely as sports highlights on Sunday, as closely as news of infamous deaths.

★ ★ ★

Thursday morning he went down to the cab company and waited in the office for a trainer to show up. The man would be an experienced cabbie who would be paid fifty dollars on top of his regular shift to train a new driver. There were three other men waiting for trainers that morning. One of them, a man named Lewis, had been in Palmer's traffic-safety course, they had sat at adjacent desks while watching the hideous accident video, so they smiled and nodded at each other like comrades, but had nothing to say. Palmer imagined that Lewis was worried about succeeding at this last of all possible jobs, was wondering, like Palmer, whether this was going to work, whether he would make enough money to live on until he figured out what to do with the rest of his life.

Palmer's trainer was a big man with red hair that looked like it could never be combed properly but only cut short. His teeth were large, the two front slightly buck. He walked up smiling with his eyebrows raised and pointed directly at Palmer as if picking a man for a shit detail. In the army this man, who introduced himself as Pemberton, would have been a sergeant E6 without any hope of promotion.

Pemberton took him outside to the parking lot, four acres of unoccupied cabs waiting for drivers. At the back of the lot rested a score of wrecks, taxis that had been involved in accidents, fenders crumpled, windshields shattered, radiators, trunks, hoods, tops, wheels flattened, a cemetery of steel bodies to be cannibalized by mechanics looking for parts unavailable on the shelves. "The first thing you do is write down your odometer mileage, and the mileage on the meter," Pemberton said, interrupting the engaging story being told by all these inert hulks.

Palmer nodded. He knew the day was going to be endless, made longer by the awkwardness of sitting for eight hours in close quarters with a stranger. Knew that he himself would never become a trainer, not even for a bonus fifty bucks.

They headed for a 7-Eleven store on Colorado Boulevard to gas up. Pemberton explained that the cab company used to sell gas on site. "They took the pumps out, but I liked it better the old way because you started the day off with a full tank. Sometimes you wonder if you're gonna make it to the gas station the way things are now." He pointed at the fuel gauge, the needle dancing on empty. "Some guys didn't like it though because the IRS could use the company's receipts to check on whether they were cheating on their income tax." Pemberton looked at Palmer. "I never cheat."

Pemberton fueled the cab and checked the oil and water while Palmer watched, then went inside and brought out two Cokes and handed one to Palmer. "All right, let's post and see what happens." Pemberton climbed into the driver's seat.

The first call of the day was to a Safeway store, an elderly lady with a shopping cart full of white plastic bags filled with groceries. The fare came to two dollars and forty cents, but Pemberton grinned as though the fare was fifty bucks as he helped the woman carry the groceries up to her door. After he got back in the car, though, Pemberton cursed and told Palmer that forty percent of the calls in this part of town were grocery stores. "You can go broke doing Safeway runs." He drove to Stapleton Airport to show Palmer the process for going through the line.

The process was remarkably civilized, a study in courtesy
and fairness and honor. The cab line was long, holding sometimes as many as eighty cabs which were hidden from the
view of the passengers at the terminal by a high concrete wall
that bordered a parking garage ramp. The line extended
along a service road near the long-term parking lots, and at
one point became a double row, the cabs waiting side-by-side
for a short stretch, so that when you pulled into the line you
had to note the number of the taxi in front of you because
things could get confused in the double line. Palmer did not
expect the system to work at all, that this juggling of idling
autos would be his ultimate downfall.

Pemberton filled him in on the hours of the day when the
cab line was moving, and when the airport was dead. "Sometimes you can wait two hours without moving. I hardly ever
work the airport myself. If you want to make decent money,
you got to take calls off the radio."

Palmer was interested in this fact because it was his plan
to do nothing but work the airport once he began driving.
When he was eighteen and had delivered furniture for a living,
he would read novels as he sat shotgun in the delivery van
steered by the various drivers who came and went that year.
Palmer read while they drove. Some of the drivers were
annoyed by this, they wanted to talk, to tell the crude sex
jokes that seemed the life's blood of truck drivers, or to discuss
their own sex lives in detail. Other drivers didn't mind his
reading, and seemed as happy tooling silently around the
city as Palmer was happy engulfed in his eclectic fiction. He
had no idea there was any difference between Jules Verne and
William Saroyan. He enjoyed any story that took him briefly
out of the truck and away from the knowledge that he would

be doing this awful work until he was drafted. His plan now was to pick up where he had left off delivering furniture. He was going to spend as much time as possible seated in his taxi at the airport, reading novels.

"They're gonna build a new international airport north of town one of these years," Pemberton said. "It's gonna kill the cab business."

Palmer nodded, but decided not to take the bad news very seriously. Every other working man he had ever met in his life viewed himself as the bearer of sobering news from some calamitous trench. It got old.

Pemberton guided the cab along the taxi chute and stopped at the terminal doors, and picked up a businessman who wanted to go to the Hilton downtown. After they dropped him off, Pemberton said ninety percent of all airport trips are to downtown hotels. That sounded fine to Palmer because the fare plus tip had come to fifteen dollars. Pemberton was beginning to collect a nice wad of green bills, which he kept tucked in his shirt pocket.

He drove down an alley a few blocks from the Hilton and pointed out a spot where a cab driver had been robbed and murdered a few months earlier. The crime had made big headlines because it was the fifth in a string of taxi robberies that had occurred in one week. The same man had committed all the robberies as well as the murder, and had been caught.

At lunchtime Pemberton drove to a Safeway where he and Palmer each bought a sandwich at the delicatessen. Palmer had never eaten a delicatessen sandwich before in his life. Delicatessens were places he saw only in movies about New York City. When he began eating his sandwich, he realized that the introduction to deli food was probably the only worthwhile part of his lessons on this day. He would be eating a lot of deli sandwiches when he finally began driving. There was nothing to this job, he could see that. Pick up fares, drop them off, take the money, eat a deli sandwich.

With only three hours left in the session Pemberton turned the driving over to Palmer. When Palmer took his place in the driver's seat he felt like he was climbing into the cockpit of an airplane. The meter, the radio, the microphone clipped to the dashboard, these were the only accouterment which differed from that which he would find in a normal car, yet it made him uneasy for all of ten minutes as he took a call from the radio, then drove to the address directed by Pemberton, who advised him to buy a map of the city.

"You're gonna make mistakes," Pemberton said with a note of satisfaction in his voice. "When I first started driving six years ago it seemed like I made a brand-new mistake every day for two months. You'll go to wrong addresses, you'll jump bells too far away to get there in time, you'll take bad checks from bums who look trustworthy, you'll pick up other driver's customers outside the mall and catch hell for it. You'll make mistakes that haven't even been invented yet. I know I did. The thing is, don't let your fuckups get you down. The day'll come when you'll go a whole week without fucking up and you'll think you got it sacked, and then one morning you'll fuck up so badly you'll think the manager's gonna tear up your license. But it won't happen. The only thing the company cares about is getting the money from you up front every morning. They don't give a fuck what you do as long as you pay for your cab."

Palmer didn't believe this last part. It sounded like the kind of horseshit you'd hear an incompetent NCO say to impress you with his knowledge of things military. Palmer believed himself capable of screwing things up so badly that he could be banned from driving any cab in the United States.

When he picked up his first customer at a seedy apartment in the suburbs, the man wanted to go only to a liquor store one mile away and return to his building. Pemberton informed the man that Palmer was a trainee, and that this was his first cab pickup ever. The customer made a joke, suggesting that he should get a discount for being driven by an amateur. Pemberton laughed. Palmer laughed too because Pemberton had explained earlier in the day that aside from chauffeuring a customer, your number one job as a driver was to be as affable as possible, because the size of your tip depended on it.

The man tipped eighty cents. Palmer got nothing. Pemberton got it all. This was how training worked. But the sight of the growing wad in Pemberton's pocket made Palmer eager to go to work for himself. Maybe the job wouldn't last, he might not make enough money, might make mistakes of such magnitude that they could never be forgiven, but he wanted badly to get started, to find out if the job might not only give him enough money to live on but might also give him hope, which he had run out of long before he'd begun running out of money.

Pemberton showed him the hotels where the cab line moved fastest, and pointed out the hotels which were to be avoided because no one ever went from there to the airport. He advised Palmer not to work the airport unless downtown was dead. Sunday was always dead, and Saturday daytime was usually slow. Saturday nights jumped when the bars started closing. Fridays were always hopping. Mondays were usually pretty good because businessmen headed out on flights. The rest of the week was fairly steady but you had to keep on the ball. "Whether you're sitting at the airport or outside a hotel, keep your radio on and be ready to jump bells. That's how you make money. A cab driver don't make money when he's sitting still. You can sit still when you get home."

Palmer appreciated the advice, even though he knew he would ignore it because he intended to become an airport rat. That's what his friend who drove for Yellow called the cabbies who not only worked the airport but who deadheaded back to the airport with an empty cab.

After seven hours on the road, Pemberton told Palmer to drive back to the cab company. After they arrived, Pemberton handed him a clipboard with a long form attached. Palmer had to critique the training. Did your trainer answer all your questions to your satisfaction? Yes. How would you rate the quality of your training, A B C D or E? A of course. Palmer gave him the highest marks, and they even shook hands when it was over. Palmer supposed that he would be seeing Pemberton around the company in the months ahead, that they might even become friends, but as with almost every assumption that Palmer had ever made in his entire life, he was wrong. He never saw Pemberton again.

WINTER

Now that he had a source of income, Palmer decided it was time he moved out of his basement apartment. He had lived there for a year after he had broken up with his last girlfriend, and it was the place where he had endured the worst of the bad dreams of his life. They were not the frightening dreams of childhood, of arms reaching out of the darkness to grab an ankle, they were dreams of anguish, contrasted with dreams of peculiar joy. He had rarely dreamed about Vietnam after he'd come home from the war, yet during the past six months he had begun having dreams where he found himself back on the army compound where he had served as a clerk/typist.

The architecture of the compound was a bit different, in the way that most familiar places are skewed in dreams, but was enough like his old duty station that he knew where he was and what was expected of him, that he would be required to spend another year in Vietnam. He stormed angrily around the compound in these dreams, exasperated that he had to do it all over again, that he had to reexperience that oppressive sense of dread that had enveloped him like a suffocating blanket during his tour twenty years ago. But oddly enough he never sought out a battalion clerk or an officer in these dreams, to explain that he had already served his year and that he was under no legal obligation to do it again. He simply accepted it as he had once accepted his real tour. He would awaken from these dreams drained from frustration, yet not especially relieved to be awake.

One night he dreamed that he was dead. The cemetery where his body was interred, the landscape itself, was made of stone. There were no lawns, no acres of empty space, only tombs rising no more than waist high and crowded together like a city which stretched into the dream distance. His tomb was right next to a large motionless body of water which extended in the opposite direction, describing a curved horizon. This tombscape was engraved with random, meandering, narrow paths, so that the living could walk among the graves. The low walls of these paths had embossed carvings of skulls, bones, and random intricate interlocking designs. He himself was dead, was a ghost floating above his tomb in a pleasant state of mind that was almost physical in its intensity, was unlike anything he had ever experienced in waking life. He drifted here and there among the tombstones, and was aware of one other ghostly presence but felt no fear or even any particular need to communicate with it. Living visitors were walking among the tombstones, families of the deceased. He felt no compulsion to draw close to them, to listen in on their conversations. He felt no particular need to do anything at all. Far across the body of water was the glow of what he thought must be a city. He neither knew nor cared, and when he awoke from this most peculiar of dreams, he kept his eyes closed and clung to its sweet ambiance as long as he could.

Whenever he dropped a passenger off in an unfamiliar neighborhood, Palmer took note of any For Rent signs he might see planted behind window glass. He would study the house or apartment building and try to imagine himself living there. He wanted some place where he could stay for a long time, a place from which he would not feel the need to flee for at least a year. He did not want to live in the suburbs, nor on Capitol Hill which had been taken over by punk rockers in the way that the heart of the city had been overrun by hippies when he had been a teenager. And he did not want to live so far away from the cab company that he would find it complicated to get there if his heap ever broke down and he had to take a bus. He did not know where he wanted to live, only that he had to get out of that awful basement apartment as soon as possible. He had the money now. This job seemed to be working.

It had not worked very well the first few shifts. He had made all the mistakes that Pemberton had warned him about, and had invented a few of his own. One day he failed to tighten the radiator cap after checking the water level, so that the water evaporated, the engine overheated and seized up, and the cab had to be towed back to the company at a cost of twenty-five dollars to Palmer, upon whom the mechanics placed the blame after discovering the loose radiator cap.

On another day he picked up a man at a bar, and then made the mistake of letting the man go into an apartment complex unescorted to "get the money." The man never came out.

On his first day of driving Palmer had earned a total of five dollars, even though he worked the maximum twelve hours. His very first fare from the airport was a cowboy who had left his truck over the weekend in the parking lot of a girls' school a few blocks from Stapleton, so that the fare was not fifteen dollars as Palmer had expected for his first trip ever out of the airport, but three dollars.

He quickly drove back to the airport and pulled up in the cab line, but not so quickly that he could outrace the sense of futility that had begun to overwhelm him. From the very outset of cab driving, from the get-go, things were not working out the way he had hoped. He was old enough to know that there was no justice in the universe, but it seemed that the odds ought to occasionally go his way through sheer caprice.

He came home that night with a fleeting sense of horror that this job was not only not going to work, it could not even be considered real. Where was that wad of long green which had made an obscene bulge in Pemberton's breast pocket? But then how many times in his life had he discovered that there was more to learning than watching someone else do it. Imitation. That word had subtle meanings that he had never appreciated until he tried doing things. Fake. Fraud. Authenticity was like a missing ingredient that he could never quite corner, capture, put to any use. If cab driving didn't work out, then he didn't know what he was going to do. But there was nothing to do except keep on trying, because the alternatives, of which there were many, were unthinkable. He had to make this work, and before winter came, he did.

On the day of the first snowfall of the season, Palmer was netting an average of sixty dollars a shift for twelve hours of driving, the same pay scale most teenagers got for flipping burgers, minus the supervision of a cranky manager, a foreman, a boss. He had enough money in the bank to begin looking in earnest for a new place to live, first and last month's rent, cleaning deposit, all the crap of paranoid landlords, although he did not realistically expect to live in a place where such things were a major concern to the live-in managers who collected rent for absentee owners. He in fact expected to live in the neighborhood of the punks and the college students going to school nights and working shit jobs in the daytime. He expected to end up on Capitol Hill.

Whenever he drove through that part of town and saw the young people in their tattered blue jeans and rock haircuts and drug jackets, he was reminded that he was forty-two years old and would not fit in, that to these young minds the Beatles were as obsolete as Tommy Dorsey had been to his own generation. Still, he contemplated the For Rent signs in the grimy windows of the buildings in that part of town as if he were looking for a room that resembled his youth.

The first snowfall was light, left only a dust of white powder on the streets, did not stick and was blown aside by the tires of passing cars. A niggling fear sprouted in Palmer's gut at this first sign of what might turn out to be an obstacle to his success. How many times in the past had he seen only cabs moving along the streets in heavy snowstorms? Up to now he had always arranged his life so that when the snow arrived and the parked cars at curbs began resembling the skyline of the Rockies he would never have to leave his apartment. Fifteen years earlier he had been fired from a job he didn't like. It primarily involved delivering carpets. Like giant redwoods those carpets were, rubber-backed and woven of artificial fibers, they made his legs bow when he and the driver trundled up sidewalks and entered the homes of pleased women who fretted as he let the monstrous weight drop on hardwood floors. It was like carrying a sofa bed on one shoulder. He did not go to work because he imagined himself slipping on an icy sidewalk, breaking a leg, a pelvis, manufacturing a hernia, all for a dollar above the minimum wage. His girlfriend had answered the phone when it rang that morning and said Palmer was too sick to come to work. His boss told her to tell Palmer not to bother coming back at all. Palmer was thirty-two years old, and the world was filled with pissed bosses.

One morning after dropping off a fare on Capitol Hill, Palmer drove past a For Rent sign planted discreetly on the large front porch of a three-story apartment building. The placard was black, the letters bright red, a sign you'd buy in a hardware store or a Woolworths. The sign caught his eye only because he became attuned to spotting obscure signs after he had begun what was turning into a rather desultory search.

The apartment was in a neighborhood which was old but not run-down. People in their late twenties and early thirties would live here, residents who held mid-level jobs—clerks, nurses, shipping-and-receiving. He backed the cab up quickly with the renegade attitude of freedom from rules that comes from driving a cab, and parked at the curb in front of the building.

Unlike the other buildings nearby with their flat tar-topped roofs, this one had a gabled roof plastered with green shingles, with one window looking out from what he assumed was an attic. The second floor had a pair of French doors that opened

onto a massive stone balcony which hid the front door of the
first floor in shadow. He got out and approached the sign,
looked for the rent price which was sometimes scribbled in
pencil on these cheap advertisements, but there was nothing
to indicate how much it would cost him to live in this place
which he felt drawn to. He knew the history of these places,
knew that they had been the homes of wealthy families
during the nineteenth century, the buildings gone to seed in
a modern world, broken up into small apartments with
jury-rigged bathrooms and kitchens the size of closets. He
went up to the front door and looked at a row of doorbells
molded in brass. He punched the bell adjacent to the word
"Manager" inscribed in blue plastic tape.

He heard footsteps approaching on a carpeted hall floor,
imagined a sprightly matron, or a man who had retired from
the military and was supplementing his pension with this
kind of work, but was surprised when a kid who could not
have been more than twenty opened the door. Fringe of dark
brown beard on his chin, dark bright eyes, he was wearing a
T-shirt and cut-off jeans, tennis shoes, looked like a college
student. Palmer was so surprised at encountering someone
who was not old that he felt as if he were speaking to an equal
and not someone twenty-two years younger than himself.

"I saw your for-rent sign," Palmer said. "Is the apartment
still available?"

"I was just heading out for a class at the free university
but I could show you the place real quick," the kid said. He
had a rapid, chortling voice, and fingered his chin as he
spoke. He led Palmer up a staircase that grew narrower as
it rose higher. Up to the second floor and then up another

staircase that was even tighter, and which took a right turn near the top. Three more steps and there was a door flush against a wall. Palmer tried to imagine how a sofa bed might be delivered to this apartment. The manager produced a chain of keys, opened the door, led him inside.

The layout of most apartments could be grasped in an instant, so whenever Palmer walked in he knew where everything was and whether or not he liked it. But when he entered this place he found himself in a small foyer with doorways leading off in different directions. The manager opened one door and said something about it being a storage room, although it was carpeted and had a window which let in strong light. The room looked as if it could serve as a nursery. They moved into the living room, which was high ceilinged and wide. This took them to the kitchen, and then into the bathroom with a tub, no shower, and Palmer began to get the sense that the place was sprawling. The small kitchen had six windows, had a door which led to the outside. The manager explained that the kitchen had been added on years ago. It was a kind of box.

Palmer went to a window and looked down. The room extended out over a dirt parking lot below. A steep fire-escape led from the door down to the scatter of parked cars owned by other tenants.

"Let me show you the bedroom," the manager said, and Palmer followed him back through the living room and into a long room facing the street, a narrow room with a low ceiling shaped like an A-frame. It was the attic he had seen from outside. There was a non-functioning fireplace in this space, was a small alcove off to the side with a desk in it, and another alcove where a shelf of books might be set up.

"How much is the rent?" Palmer asked only because he had to, because he was dazzled by this aerie, and knew from past experience that the price would be too high.

"Two-forty a month," the young man replied, the chortle disappearing now that they were discussing financial matters. "I know that sounds cheap, but the thing is, the owners want steady renters who are gonna stick around for a long time. They don't want someone who's just gonna throw a mattress on the floor and eat out of tin cans. If you're interested in renting the place, they'll want to know about your background and what kind of work you do and all that."

He didn't seem to be trying to discourage Palmer. Palmer sensed that the kid did not dislike him, that his being a tenant would be acceptable to this manager whose job it was to pass first judgment on the strangers who came to his door, an occupation similar to being a cab driver, but with its own unique intensities.

"I can bring you a deposit later today," Palmer said. "I can bring cash if you want."

"That would be good," the kid said, the chortle returning to his voice. "Cash up front always makes a good impression on the owner."

When Palmer got back into his cab he felt an excitement and a craving he had not known in years. He wanted that apartment, could not imagine anything as great as living in that crow's nest in the sky. He went to get the deposit money out of his bank, and as he drove, half-listening to the calls being offered on the radio, he considered just what he would write in the one-page resume about himself that the manager had suggested he produce as soon as possible.

"I left home at the age of eighteen," he said aloud to the voice of the dispatcher flowing ceaselessly out of the speaker, "and got a job delivering furniture. I was eventually drafted into the army. I served one year in Vietnam and returned home where I entered college on the GI Bill. I earned a Bachelor of Arts Degree in English. After that I held a variety of jobs . . ."

This first part was easy to voice impromptu because it had the quality of a short story in which there is only so much room to describe what happened but very little space for in-depth explanations, whys, wherefores, justifications, apologies, excuses. When he got as far as leaving the drunken Eden of academia and taking his place in the real world, the mental pen with which he wrote all first drafts faltered. Most of the jobs he had held had been meaningless shit, and a few were actually painful to remember. There seemed nothing he had done since college worth mentioning in a resume, and as he approached the bank he realized that the biographical information he was obliged to write for the owner of the apartment building might end up taking the shape—like the taxi cemetery behind the cab company—of a motley collection of rather badly dented truths.

That night Palmer sat down in front of his typewriter to begin fabricating his resume. He decided that while he would not lie to the apartment owner, he would provide a patina of facts that may or may not hold up under serious questioning. He mentioned that he was a producer of public access TV shows, although he had not done any shows of this sort in more than three years. He mentioned his military record. And he listed only the jobs he had not been fired from, although this cut his work references almost in half.

He had done some freelance writing in his late thirties, in a last effort to wring some practical use from his English degree. Like most English majors, he had attempted to write novels, and like most English majors, he had failed to produce anything publishable. He had gotten technical writing jobs through friends and acquaintances, and a thin network of business connections. He had written a brochure for one man, producing a two-page pamphlet extolling the benefits of professional financial planning, only to realize that the man was a fraud, an insurance agent who simply wanted to foist lifetime policies off on gullible customers.

In his mid-thirties he had worked at three separate jobs in the publications department of private corporations. What he had in mind at the time, as his novel-writing ambitions had begun to wither, was working his way into a job as a staff writer on a local city magazine. At some point between the age of twenty-five and thirty-five he had begun to realize that almost all of his life ambitions were never going to be realized. He knew he was never going to become a filmmaker, which had been a kind of vague dream of his when he was young, but which had been supplanted by a stronger desire to become a novelist. And then in his thirties, while attempting to write screenplays as often as novels, he found himself applying for jobs in publication departments of corporations. But he found something to dislike about each of the jobs. Editors who had no respect for his copy. Editors who made excruciating changes in the blue lines. Office managers who had no respect for the wisdom of editors. Owners who came in from lunch with rum on their breath and decided to throw out whole articles one day before the printer's deadline. It was only after he had given up on these futile forays into the world of pseudo-journalism that it occurred to him that what he really disliked about the jobs was wearing a suit.

No matter how he tried to couch this graphic history of his life and jobs in glowing terms, he could not avoid mentioning on his thin resume that what he did for a living at the moment was drive a taxicab, earning three hundred dollars a week. This, of course, was a lie. To earn that much he would have had to work five days a week, and he had found that he was physically incapable of working even two days in a row. Sitting in a cab for twelve hours, sometimes not getting out for three or four hours at a stretch, was brutal. He would never have believed that a body which had always been so attuned to sitting in front of a television could be poleaxed by a job that required virtually no motion whatsoever.

He mentioned the flower delivery job that he had held when he was nineteen because there was something seemingly noble about the occupation. A man who once had delivered flowers is a man who will pay his rent on time. The job lasted less than a month, but it wasn't the prospect of seeing corpses that made him quit. He realized the job was coming to an end the day his boss handed him a spray of roses painted jet-black and told him to deliver them to a house in the suburbs. Palmer didn't understand why the roses had been painted black, and didn't ask, but on the way to the house he took a peek at the card which was tucked inside an unsealed envelope.

The message was vicious, castigating a woman who had broken up a marriage.

Palmer didn't want to carry this terrible bouquet up to the door, ring the bell, and hand it to the woman who had stolen a married man, but he did it. When the door opened, a middle-aged woman peered out at him questioningly. He handed her the roses and mumbled something about them being for her. He turned and walked quickly back to his van, climbed in, and drove away, and knew that he was going to be looking for a new job.

He drove back to the apartment building, but the manager was not in. He had said something about attending a class in either yoga or macramé. Palmer slipped the resume under the door and drove back to his apartment feeling as he had felt when he used to submit short stories to literary magazines, dropping an envelope off at the post office and then driving home and casually looking into his mailbox before going inside.

The next day he stayed home from work because whenever he was expecting something, an important letter or bad news or an acceptance slip, he tended to drop the business of Life. On the day that he had opened his draft notice he had decided to quit work at the ice cream company right then, though was still intimidated enough by the adult world to call in the next morning and tell them he was quitting. He had some pay coming. It would be another six weeks before he was inducted. By the time it no longer mattered, he barely had ten dollars to his name.

That afternoon the manager called and told him he could have the apartment. "I think the owner was swayed by the front money," the kid said, his laughter bubbly on the phone.

After Palmer hung up, a sense of dreaminess engulfed him. It was as though he had won a contest whose odds were virtually insurmountable. By dint of moderate effort he had obtained the worst job and the best apartment he'd ever had, except he knew now that cab driving was not the worst job he'd ever had. Now that he had gotten past the mistakes of the novice and was making sixty and on rare occasion as much as one hundred dollars per shift, he was beginning to realize that cab driving was not only not the worst job conceivable, it was in fact the only good job he'd ever held.

When it had first occurred to him to become a cab driver, his knowledge of the profession had come from the movies, and from tales told by his friend who drove for Yellow, and the sight of cab drivers in their grubby clothing hoisting suitcases into trunks outside hotels. It had seemed a shabby and hopeless life, yet now it was as if some secret was slowly being revealed to him. Though he made far less money than he had on any other job—he had made twenty grand a year as a staff writer for an in-house magazine—he had never felt as contented as he did now when he took his place in the driver's seat which was analogous to the office desks where he had spent hours doing nothing but trying to look busy while salesmen sipped from paper cups around the Mr. Coffee and told each other how crucial they were to the industry as a whole.

He immediately set about packing for the move, stuffing laundry, clean and dirty, into pillowcases, and placing dishes and silverware in a box which had accompanied him on all such moves for the past twenty years. The dishes had been a birthday gift from one of his girlfriends. She had given them to him before they had moved in together, and he had taken them with him after she told him the time had come for the two of them to decide what they wanted to do with their lives.

Wasn't much to pack. He had learned to travel light in the army, one worthwhile lesson he'd gleaned from those two years. He had brought very little to this basement apartment, which he had always considered a temporary way-station to better things, and had ended up staying for two years. Stasis. But what more could a man ask for than a place to put down roots and die surrounded by strangers? He was ready to load his car and drive over to the apartment right now, but the manager had told him he couldn't come for the keys until after five p.m. the next day.

Palmer went out and visited a few Salvation Army stores which stocked used television sets. He had not owned a TV for more than a year, and he missed it in spite of the fact that he had gotten along so far without it. He saw color TVs for as low as sixty dollars, and massive black-and-white TVs for less than a hundred. He was going to move into a third-story apartment, to live on a height, to see more of the sky than the city when he looked out a window, and he felt he was going to be there for a long time, and a man who is going to be any-where for a long time needs a TV.

He didn't see anything he liked at the stores, but it didn't matter. Just the act of going out to find a television set, making a significant change in his life, pleased him, and when he returned to his basement apartment that night he decided he would work a short-shift at the cab company the next day and be ready to go for the keys to his aerie at five p.m. Driving would fill his day and stifle the restlessness bred always by new horizons. His impatience would be cured by labor's numbing panacea.

Snow began falling during the night, and there was an inch on the roads when Palmer went out to warm up his heap. Brushing the residue off the windshield, puffing from stretching and exertion, he felt robust, felt ready to tackle what promised to be a good day, for snow is a cab driver's best friend — when the weather is bad, people leave their cars in garages, abandon plans of taking a bus downtown, dial the phone for taxi service, the radio is always jumping. You have your pick of the good trips, the airport trips, you don't have to settle for grocery runs like dregs on the bottom of a slow day.

He drove to the company and paid for an eight-hour short lease for one of only three available cars. Everyone was working today, and he knew there would be someone waiting for his cab at the end of the day. The drivers' room was crowded with men stamping snow off their feet and tossing scarves around their necks, the parking lot filled with laughing men in boom times clutching trip sheets and brushing drifts off their windshields and heading out into the storm. Palmer took his key and trip sheet and went out to the parking lot to search for his cab, trying to contain the undeniable feeling of camaraderie that had been generated within him by all this vehicular exuberance, like a bright spot in a disaster, like the army sometimes had been, like life should always be. His car was one of the newer taxis in the fleet, ex-police cruiser modified for hacking purposes by the men in the garage. It started right up, the windshield wipers worked, the cleaning-fluid reservoir was full, there was a quarter tank of gas left over from the driver who had probably turned the cab in early the previous evening, perhaps demoralized by the coming of the snow too late during his own shift.

Palmer drove out of the lot and headed toward the heart of Denver, the blower transforming his vehicle into a wad of heat that would be appreciated by businessmen hailing cabs at hotels. He felt that the day could not be more perfect, that this job could not be more perfect, that though he had always believed that every decision he had ever made was wrong, he had stumbled through desperation and blind luck into the job that had been waiting for him all his life.

He pulled in at the Hilton, but the line was moving so fast that he barely had time to fill in the boilerplate on his trip sheet before a man carrying a briefcase got into the cab and said, "The History Museum," rather than "Airport" which was what almost all businessmen said out of the Hilton. The museum at City Park was a six-dollar trip at best. But even this did not diminish the pleasure the day was giving Palmer. Lousy trips often led to surprisingly good trips, even trips out of town, which meant there was no reason to get angry about a short trip, unless the day was ending and you had barely paid off your cab lease.

It was not a wet snow coming down on the city but a dry one which blew off the streets where the traffic was heavy.

Palmer dropped his fare off at the museum, then pulled out onto Colorado Boulevard to get back downtown to the hotels. The road was icy here, the pavement sloping gently downhill to 17th Avenue half a mile away. He slowed when he saw the light turn red up ahead, and in his slowing he lost control of the car.

It came on him instantly, a gentle pinch of terror making his arms weak as he tried to steer the car which would not obey because the wheels were sliding on a sheet of black ice. He began tapping the brakes as one is taught to do when sixteen and going for a learner's permit, recalling with contradictory calm those bits of advice you get from friends and driver's ed movies, steer into the slide, tap brakes, maintain control, but there was something tremendously wrong here.

He glanced into the rear-view mirror and saw a city bus behind him which was successfully slowing, the driver apparently aware that the taxi in front of him was in trouble and was giving it plenty of room for the inevitable crash. In front of Palmer there seemed to be an entire parking lot of cars waiting for the red light to change to green, and as his taxi slid toward the rear of the nearest car, the thought passed through his mind that he was about to have his first traffic accident ever in a taxi. He had always supposed that an accident would take place sooner or later, that the odds went that way when you toted up thousands of miles over the months. He now accepted it, but felt bad for the person in the driver's seat perhaps fifty feet ahead of him. Innocent person trying to get to work. For some reason, he thought a woman was at the wheel.

The cars ahead of him began to move forward. The light had turned green. By the time Palmer was twenty feet away from the woman's car they were both traveling the same rate of speed, and distance between them ceased closing. After a few moments, the cars ahead of him were actually pulling away while his taxi continued to slide down the gentle slope of Colorado Boulevard toward 17th, changing lanes of its own accord, moving off to the right, with the pressure of the tires bumping at last against the curb and bringing the brief and frightening journey to a rattling end.

He quickly looked into the mirror, afraid now of being rear-ended, but all he saw was the bus and a line of cars perhaps a hundred feet behind him, all of them having stopped. He had been their dog-and-pony show, a disaster they could describe to people in the office later in the morning or to their families at night when they got home. But they had not gotten their money's worth.

He touched his chest. Three or four hearts were beating behind his ribs, each at its own rate. He couldn't quite get his breath. He felt light-headed, felt as if he might have to lie down on the front seat. His mind was already replaying the movie of that near miss, the cars suddenly moving away from him, velocity like an accordion, the sort of luck you have only in dreams.

He knew he could not drive the rest of the day. He would have to take the cab back and suffer whatever penalty the company demanded. Probably the loss of his lease money. He put the car into gear, eased slowly down to 17th, turned right, and ended up taking side streets back to the cab company. As he guided the taxi carefully along the frosty streets, apprehensive at every empty intersection, all he could think about was the long winter ahead of him, and the rent

money he would be obligated to hand over to the apartment
manager on the first of every month, and the fact that this job
may not work out after all, and that every decision he had
ever made was wrong.

Thanksgiving came and went. Holidays were slow. Palmer
learned the true meaning of hope when he found himself
refusing to think about finding some other kind of work even
though there would be snow off and on with its ambush
black ice until the middle of March. He had learned the meaning of hope in the way a rock climber scaling a vertical wall
of stone realizes in a tight spot that he can go only up, that
down is not an option. There was no other work that Palmer
could do. He did not have the capacity to do anything for
money other than sit for hours and stare through a pane of
tinted glass. He had already quit all the jobs he was capable
of starting.

  He would have quit the army after one week if they
wouldn't have come after him with guns and badges. He had
announced the quitting of some jobs ahead of time, but that
was when he was young, was still pretending to be a grown-
up in that he tried to do things the way he thought an adult
would do them, like giving two weeks' notice. I owe them
that much, he used to tell himself, feeling rather noble about
his courtesies to the owners of factories or small shops who
could not have cared less if he quit or lived or died a miserable
death. Then he developed a system of picking up his final
paycheck on a Friday and never showing up for work again.

This was when he began to understand the charm of not answering his phone.

When he moved into his aerie he decided he would not have a telephone, because there was not one person left in the city whom he wanted to talk to, although more significantly, there was not one person left in the city who wanted to talk to him.

He did not end up moving into the apartment, as he had intended, on the day of the terrifying slide. He knew that it was his eagerness to move things forward at a fast pace that had led to his driving a short shift that day, so that after he turned the cab in he went back to his apartment and slept, got up and finished packing, then slept again and did not go to his new place until the following day, when the ice had melted, the sun was out, and his depression had peaked.

How many times in his life had his wrong decisions consisted of doing things too quickly? Talking to women. Falling for sales pitches. Buying clothes. Appliances. Off-brand wines. When he was young his bad decisions seemed counterbalanced by an abundance of Time. But his willingness to take risks was now counterbalanced by an overbearing history of failure. How many times had he screwed up to the point that his decisions could no longer be rationalized as the optimism of youth, but were revealed to be simple incompetence? At some point in his late thirties he realized that he no longer trusted himself.

On the day of his slide on the ice, the cab company had given him his lease money back. They told him that the mechanics had not gotten snow tires put onto all the vehicles, and that other men had returned their cars complaining about sliding around on the streets too. Palmer had taken his money home believing that he might never drive a cab again, that he could not make it through a winter worrying about ice. But after he brought all of his things to his new place, had locked the door shut, had sat in the kitchen listening to the gentle rattling hum of the refrigerator turning off and on, he knew he had to make cab driving work because there was nothing else he could do.

This became a kind of mantra that he muttered as he went about setting up his things. "There's nothing else I can do. There's nothing else I can do." He mumbled it while cooking dinner, while sitting in the bathtub with a washcloth over his eyes. "There's nothing else I can do." And as with the cosmic powers traditionally ascribed to mantras, the chant had its effect. He calmed down, and decided that he would drive only when the weather was good. That patch of ice was probably an anomaly. He would pay attention to the weather reports every night from now on, as would a farmer, a pilot, a sailor at sea.

The second night in his new apartment he drove to another Salvation Army store and looked over the selection of used televisions. He ended up buying a black-and-white for seventy dollars. He drove home and carried it upstairs carefully, as if it were some sort of magic icon that would protect him at work, and after he plugged it in and adjusted the aerial he waited eagerly for the news, weather, and sports to come on at ten—waited, he thought, as the Greeks must have waited for the Oracle at Delphi to field their questions.

"What's the weather going to be?"

Partly cloudy with a ten percent chance of flurries. Later on in the week a low front will be moving in from the west bringing with it a bit of moisture. The National Weather

Bureau in Washington D.C. is predicting a white Christmas. Stay tuned for sports highlights.

He drove two days later when the sun had come out and the snow had melted and the air was as warm as if winter had passed. The sunlight was blinding, a summer sun, he drove a full shift on the dry streets, and the uneasiness that he had anticipated was not there. The curbs were white with salt laid down by city trucks to melt the snow, but he might have been driving in June. At the end of the day he turned his cab in confident that things were going to work out.

The next morning the sky was low with gray clouds, looked snow heavy, so he didn't drive. The air was cold but not freezing, and it reminded him of his college days when he used to take a bus to UCD for night courses, walking in weather like this, heavy coat, scarf, knit hat, books lugged under one arm, creative writing courses, the Spanish they made him take even though he was majoring in English. Then meeting with other students after class in a small 3.2 bar converted from a Victorian house. They sat outside at concrete tables in the autumn evenings, until the season became too cold to drink beer out of doors. In the winter they drank inside the Victorian building amid its odors of popcorn and varnish, waiting for nothing more than spring to come so they could sit outside in their short sleeves and sunglasses.

So he did not drive that day. He was now letting nature make his decisions for him. The names of the weekdays ceased to have any meaning. He drove only when the weather looked promising, though sometimes he was caught up in snowstorms that came over the city late in the afternoons. He always thought of turning his cab in then, motivated by the memory of that awful slide which would always be fresh in his mind, but instead he just watched the streets closely, examined the thin layers of snow on the asphalt, watched for ice, until he understood that it actually had been an anomaly, the weather had been odd that day, snow melting and then freezing, turning the boulevards into skating rinks. Monday, Saturday, Wednesday, Sunday—it didn't matter what day it was. Only the weather mattered.

He never knew what he would find on TV because the programming changed on weekends and the only programs he watched with any regularity were the weather reports. He was appalled, after only a year of not watching TV, at how bad the sitcoms had become. Nothing seemed to be produced on film anymore, it was all video-taped on one set with an audience providing background laughter for unfunny gags. The television shows of his youth were epic in ambition, miniature movies—what would it cost to produce Sugarfoot nowadays, and who would go to the trouble anyway when the sponsors were making artistic decisions?

He could not remember television being so bad. Had his parents hated TV when he was a boy, as he hated it now? Rock music was awful nowadays, but had the music of his generation been as awful to his parents? *Rolling Stone* occasionally reports the demise of bands he had never heard of. Dick Clark hawks the greatest hits of the Eighties. Is this what growing old is like? Is this something he had not been told about, that as you grow older you come to despise everything indiscriminately?

★ ★ ★

Friday was Palmer's favorite day, the day he made the most money, the day that temporarily shrank his economic worries, a hundred bucks practically guaranteed, almost half his rent garnered on a single day. Every driver was in it for the money and everyone had their own strategies. Airport. Downtown. Hotels. Radio. Every driver had his own approach, his own part of town, his own theories about the longest trips and the biggest tips. Some drivers refused to work the bars, other drivers worked only the bars, hauling home drunks who tipped well because alcohol bred largesse.

But Palmer simply went wherever he could find money. He learned for himself that working only the airport did not work at all. You cannot deadhead to the airport every time you drop someone off at the Hilton downtown, you've got to get in line and take a businessman back to the airport or you won't make a profit. But you were not guaranteed a trip back to the airport. You might end up at Cherry Creek. Or the line might be slow that day, but this was never a problem on Fridays. On Fridays Palmer was a shuttlecock, Hilton to the airport, airport to the Hilton, or Holiday Inn, or the Sheraton, so that he felt no sense of loss or guilt or worry when he would pull into the airport line and turn off the radio and pull out a paperback and settle in for an hour of reading while the cabs pulled forward one space every five minutes until it was time to travel down the chute and pick up passengers who had flown in from out of state and always seemed glad to have survived another flight on a deregulated airline.

On a Friday afternoon in December, one week before Christmas, Palmer pulled into the cab line just as a light snow began to fall. The morning had started as clear as a summer day, but by noon a cold easterly had brought in low clouds which blanketed his windshield with snowflakes as he sat reading. The air inside the taxi itself began to cool down noticeably. The notion that he ought to turn his cab in early came to mind but he squelched it, understanding that his slide on the ice had generated within him a nervous tick, a false warning flag that would have to be removed willfully if he was ever going to make this job work.

The cabs ahead of him began to creep forward. He started his engine and followed them. Three spaces. Three cabs had traveled down the chute and picked up passengers in the terminal which was hidden from view by the ramp which led up to the parking garage. He shut off the engine and settled in to read his book, glancing up every now and then to see if the cabs ahead were moving, and to watch the progress which was being made by the light snow which had begun again to gather in tiny drifts along the edges of his windshield wipers.

The sight of flakes slowly stacking sent him into the sort of reverie he had always gotten from watching a wood fire. Hypnotic. Forty-two winters, not counting the hot winter of Vietnam. Twenty years ago. He was only twenty-one when he arrived there. All his buddies were probably married now and had kids who could have died in any of the recent wars that were no more than battles but had to be called wars for the winners. His youth was not lost to time but had simply been shunted aside by people younger than himself. No wonder his parents' generation had hated beatniks, hippies, the flood of punks obliterating the honor earned in the Second World War and the endurance of the Depression in the

Thirties. All glory is not fleeting but upstaged by newer, less interesting glory.

The flakes began to get bigger and to fall a bit faster, and again he thought about quitting early and turning in his cab. He had already earned his lease payoff, but had made no profit yet. The line had been moving forward every five minutes, and he had made it halfway to the entrance of the chute. Maybe ten cabs ahead of him. He decided to go ahead and make one last airport run and then quit. Fifteen dollars downtown would give him something for this day's work, and you never knew, sometimes you got a fifty-dollar trip to the southwest corner of the metro-area, the new subdivisions where aging yuppies had put down their nylon roots.

He began reading again, losing himself in the story and forgetting about money and the motion of the cabs, forgetting about the snow that continued to fall, building up at the base of his windshield which he would wipe away the next time the cabs moved forward. The wind picked up, he could hear it sailing through the rails that bordered the ramp overhead, could see snow being blown off the hood of his cab. With the wind came larger flakes, the kind that would pile up fast covering the ice on the streets, so that he knew he could make this last run safely.

The wind died down and the flakes that had been blowing horizontally in the biggest gusts were now settling vertically onto his hood. Men had been standing out in the storm talking, ignoring the snow, but now it had become too heavy and everyone had gotten into their cabs which, because the line had not moved for nearly half an hour, were beginning to look like the skyline of the Rockies. Engines were running, heaters warming legs, tailpipes emitting spiraling vapors. Palmer started his engine, hit the wipers, looked at his gas gauge which was half empty. He would be turning the cab in with a good load of fuel for the next driver.

He let the engine idle for ten minutes, then shut it off to a silence so thick that he rolled his window down and listened. The silence was odd, something was missing, then he realized it was the unabated sound of jet engines roaring beyond the terminal, out on the runways. He kept the window open for five minutes, listening, until the interior of the cab began to chill. He rolled up the window and started his engine and turned the heater on full blast.

He tried to read, but kept looking up from his paperback to the entrance of the chute that ran beneath the parking ramp, kept glancing at it as if he expected the first car in line to shake off its snow and head for the terminal. Waited as if he expected an explanation to avail itself, which it did. A man in a dark blue uniform walked out of the chute and approached the first cab. The driver rolled down his window, snow dropping in clumps off the ledge onto the uniformed man's boots. The men spoke briefly, then the uniformed man, an airport security guard, moved along to the next car and spoke to the driver. The guard approached each cab and spoke, and when he got to Palmer's cab the window was already down.

"There's no planes coming in right now," the man said. "The runways are closed. They're clearing the snow off but they don't know when any planes will be coming in. It'll be at least an hour, maybe longer. Flights are being diverted to Dallas."

Having imparted his bad news, the man walked to the
next cab in line. Palmer rolled up his window and sat in the
silence thinking about his profits. Then, one by one, the cabs
ahead of him began pulling away, making U-turns and heading back to the service road which would take them toward
downtown. Where there had been ten cars ahead of him,
there were now only three. Palmer started his engine and
pulled up, closed the gap, and shut off the engine.

After an hour, the other cabs ahead of him had left.
Palmer was parked at the entrance to the chute where he got
out and scraped two inches of snow off his hood. There were
no cabs behind him. He was the entire cab line. He got back
in and turned on the heater until he was warm again, then
shut it off and cracked his window and listened for the sound
of jets that might have braved the snow which continued to
fall leaving bare only the high gray wall of the ramp on his
left where the wind twisted the snow at its base building
tent-like drifts, then dismantling them and reassembling
them further along the path of the now buried road.

SPRING

March was Palmer's least favorite month because it was the time of year when major changes always seemed to happen in his life, right around St. Patrick's Day, although the holiday itself did not have any particular significance in this schematic. March was the month he had moved away from home at the age of eighteen. March was the month when he had been drafted. March was the month he had returned from Vietnam and received his discharge papers and got on a bus and rode through the damp streets of Seattle and stared out his window at passing dark rich green lawns. March was the month he had applied to go to college on the GI Bill, and barely made it under the wire to take the required ACT test. March was the month he had left the most women, moving out after noisy fights or the worst fights of all, the silent ones. March was the month he had dropped out of college because he couldn't stand it anymore, only to go back to school two years later, to CU Denver, when it finally occurred to him that he could start living off his unused GI Bill benefits again and would not have to work or worry about money for a while.

March, the month of Spring, signaled the end of things for Palmer. He felt that if this cab driving job was not going to work out, it would end in March, a few days on either side of St. Pat's. Something would happen to throw the fragile balance of his life out of kilter and force him to look for other work. It reminded him of the unpleasant anticipation he had experienced in Vietnam knowing that he would have to get on a plane for a fifteen-hour flight home, because at that time of his life he despised flying.

The lessening of his fear of flying over the years was a mystery. By the time he was in his thirties and working for corporations that flew employees to distant locations for conventions, he found that he did not need to drink alcohol to calm his nerves during a flight. Peering out a window after takeoff, watching the houses and highways shrink to unrecognizability, he found it pleasant to be so high above the earth in a machine designed to do just that. He wondered whether his fear of flying had diminished because, unlike when he was young, he did not feel there would be all that much to lose if the plane went down.

As March approached, Palmer could measure the progress of the tilt of the earth by his watch, each Friday the sun rising just a bit earlier than the previous Friday. In December and January he would find himself at six-thirty a.m. sitting outside a hotel reading a paperback by the beam of a small penlight. In February the light at that hour was gray and he could make out the print. No more purchasing batteries at 7-Eleven where he bought gasoline and Coca-Cola and snacks in the morning. No more gripping the steel shell of the penlight with gloved fingers. Was that roughing it or what? There were so many things about cab driving that were like the army, and something as simple as reading a book by penlight in a frigid dawn reminded him of basic training where he was always out of doors and never allowed to sit down, and when he did sit down he fell asleep instantly. The drill sergeants would yell. How he wished he could still fall asleep instantly. He had lain awake nights all through the winter, unable to stop worrying about money, about whether this job was going to last, and wondering what he would do if it didn't.

Furniture delivery. He could do that again. But he was in no shape to handle sofa beds on steep stairs. Technical writing for a corporation. But he was in no shape to handle office politics. Before he had become a corporate writer he had thought office politics was just a joke, something you'd see in a Tony Randall comedy. But when he discovered for himself the existence of office politics he also discovered that it was not, unlike in Tony Randall movies, funny. The sorts of people who worked for corporations, who enjoyed wearing suits and ties, the women in pant-suits, were beyond his comprehension. No one spoke standard English. They spoke in phrases— phraseology—that seemed drawn from corporate manuals. But was this not like the army where jargon reigned? He had been relieved to find that the amount of jargon used at the cab company ran to a minimum. The cab drivers did not seem interested in that esoteric aspect of working. The majority of the drivers seemed to Palmer not unlike himself, driving a cab was a transition job, something to do until something better came along in their lives.

He hadn't expected to find himself hanging out with the groups of men who gathered every day in the airport line, leaving their cars unattended while they shot the shit and waited for the snack truck to make its afternoon run. Now he got out each day and approached men with whom he had a nodding acquaintance. He was amazed one afternoon to hear two men discussing writing.

They were both younger than him, in their late twenties, one of them sitting in the open door of a cab and another standing, looking at a sheaf of paper in his hand. A short story perhaps, some bit of serious literary business under discussion. How many times in college had Palmer witnessed this scene, two or more students bent to a piece of writing, tortoise-shell glasses dark to match their frowns, cheeks sucked in, the appropriateness of a verb or the inexcusability of an adjective mulled over, crossed off. And how many times had he been one of these students, wondering if the short story for which he had just received an A+ in a creative writing class might be of sufficient artistic and professional quality to submit to the editor of a literary magazine. How he and his friends had frowned upon the slicks, the Playboys and Esquires, yet how they had dreamed of slipping one past the slush piles and selling out. Palmer couldn't help it. He intruded on the conversation bluntly by asking if these two drivers wrote fiction.

"I'm trying," the seated man said. The other man was not a writer but had offered to read a few things written by his buddy.

"Do you write?" they both said.

It had been a long time since anyone had asked Palmer this, and his instinct was to say yes. But he stopped himself from asserting that at one time he wrote fiction, even tried screenplays, and chose to go with the cleanest truth. "I wrote some stuff in college," he replied. "I never published anything. I was an English major."

In this way he was brought into their conversation, insofar as they did not snub him. He stood and listened while they discussed a novel that the seated man was writing. He'd produced only sixty pages so far, and wondered aloud if this was enough to submit to a literary agent.

The conversation grew stale at this point for Palmer. He had heard it all before, the speculation about agents, how one goes about finding one, what agents were looking for, and whether a novel ought to be completed before contacting one. He was amused by the phrase "contacting an agent," as if you simply dialed one up and informed him that your manuscript was ready to be shipped to Scribner's. In fact Palmer found the conversation painful to listen to, like sitting through an intolerable rerun of a movie that mocked everything you ever believed in. He told the writer good luck and went to the snack truck that had just pulled in.

He bought a can of Coke and drifted back toward the line of cabs, and stopped to listen to a group of men discussing some political intrigue taking place at another cab company which was owned by the drivers, a co-op. It seemed like there was always an election in the air, a score of men vying for some obscure office. Men in greasy blue jeans and untucked shirts and unkempt beards looking to build a power base, collaring drivers at the snack truck and asking if they had voted yet.

Two men standing by a cab were joking about something, and Palmer thought he heard the army mentioned, and just as he was always interested in conversations about writing, so too was he drawn to talk of the army. In some way that he did not understand, he had never quite come to grips with the fact that he had been in Vietnam. Something seemed unresolved in his mind, something he felt could only be clarified by talking to others who had served. Perhaps it was nothing more than the uneasy feeling that the experience had been so unreal that he needed to find out from others if their experiences also possessed that unreal quality.

The man who had mentioned the army held a striking resemblance to Burl Ives, was chubby, had a white goatee.

"Are you a veteran?" Palmer asked.

The man looked at him and nodded twice quickly.

"Did you serve in Vietnam?"

"Nope. I was out by then. I served in World War Two."

Palmer was astonished by this statement. That a man who had served in his father's war should be driving a cab seemed tragic. The man didn't look as old as Palmer's father, and probably wasn't. Is this what being forty-two years old meant, that a man who ought to seem ancient did not?

"Where were you stationed?" Palmer said.

"My unit went into Formosa," the man replied. He leaned back against the cab with his arms folded. "I spent a year in Japan after the war ended."

"Were you Infantry?"

"Combat engineers."

Palmer nodded, but couldn't think of anything else to ask. Had the man long ago, even before Palmer was born, tired of talking about his stretch in the service? Palmer had never met anyone who showed the least interest in his own year in Vietnam. Nobody had ever asked him about the only interesting thing that had ever happened to him in his life. Nobody had ever wanted to know exactly what he had done during that year, not even any of his relatives. The army itself, war itself, was something only little kids seemed to find intriguing, boys curious to match up reality with the things they'd seen in movies. Palmer could remember only one man, a co-worker in a graphics shop, who had been curious about his experience in Vietnam. The man claimed to be a World War II buff, but when Palmer informed him that he had been only a clerk/typist and not a grunt in Vietnam, the man lost interest. War is about the Infantry. If you weren't in combat, you weren't in the war.

The taxis began moving forward, ending the conversation. Everyone got into their cabs to pull up four spaces. When the line ceased to move, they got out to resume interrupted conversations about sports and politics but Palmer remained inside his cab, sipping at his Coke and wondering about the veteran, until he realized that what he really had wanted to ask him was how old he was, and how had life brought him to this place at this time, operating a hack.

He tried not to think about this, sifting through a sheaf of paperwork at his side and pulling out the monthly newsletter which had been distributed at the company that morning, a stack left in the drivers' room. It was a quick read. News briefs. Admonitions to drive safely. Ninety-six days without an accident. People whom he didn't know had been promoted to jobs he didn't understand. What is a comptroller? The cheap artwork was the same in all the newsletters. There was a cartoon driver seated in a cartoon cab at a red light. Not very well-drawn, but ambitious, as all amateur artwork is. He himself had a one-page essay published in a student literary magazine during his freshman year in college, and when he first opened the magazine he became so excited that a disinterested bystander might have thought he was going to get paid.

★ ★ ★

Palmer stayed home for two days in a row, took an extra day off, and on the third day leased a cab at dawn. He went to the airport as he always did at the beginning of each shift, and watched for the veteran, thinking about talking with him again. A man who had served in WWII might be able to resolve the residual unreality of Vietnam. But he didn't see the man that day, and this didn't surprise him. There were hundreds of drivers in the city from four different taxi companies, and the turnover was high. Men came and went, hired on and quit, found that driving didn't meet whatever needs they had, the support of a family, a drug habit, alcohol, or simply getting by. He'd had a fare one day, a middle-aged black woman, who told him that she used to drive a cab but had finally quit. "I need a steady paycheck, honey," she said. She showed him the quickest route to her destination, even telling him to speed up at one point to make a light that always changed too soon. The ex-cab drivers he picked up now and then always insisted on sitting shotgun.

He didn't drive on St. Patrick's Day. Holidays were dead, like Sundays. The following Monday was the first day of spring, and he leased a cab and drove to the airport and got in a long line that didn't budge for almost an hour. Strange for a Monday, but patterns could never really be relied on. It seemed like he spent half his time trying to psyche-out the marketplace. What can I do to increase my daily take? Maybe I shouldn't work the airport. Maybe I should take more calls off the radio. But every time he tried to give himself an edge, implement a strategy, find the place in the city where the radio was jumping, it never panned out. He was destined to earn sixty bucks a day no matter what, and he knew it.

The sound of engines starting up told him the line was about to move. He put down his paperback and started his engine. Always exciting when the cab line moved, as if the whole lot of them were going to run through the chute and pick up ski fares to Aspen. Go home flush. Retire from driving altogether.

Three cabs entered the chute, and the cabs at the head of the line crept forward to fill up the empty spaces, but the cab in front of Palmer did not move. A ridiculous kind of impatience overcame him, an eagerness to pull forward three spaces. He let the man sit idle for a minute, then hit his horn once to get him moving. Cabs behind him began honking a choir of impatience, and Palmer hopped out and hurried up to the cab in front of him. The driver's window was open. It was the WWII veteran, and he was asleep. Palmer reached in and tapped the man on the shoulder, and his hand jerked back as though the tips of his fingers had been burned. The driver's flesh was stiff. There was an odor in the cab, the sweet stink that Palmer had been told about in Vietnam but had never smelled. The man's jaw was parted and a thin string of spittle hung straight down from his lower lip to his chest where a stain like a bullet wound had formed. Heart attack. Stroke. The cabs at the rear of the line continued honking, but Palmer did not wave them off, did not go to them and tell them what had happened.

He walked back to his cab and called the dispatcher. By the time he finished explaining what had happened, other men, angry at first, had gathered around the window where the dead man sat with his head bowed. During the time it took for a taxi supervisor, a tow truck, and an ambulance to arrive, the cabs at the front of the line had crept forward another ten spaces, but Palmer had not pulled his cab up, as though to drive around the dead man's cab would be disrespectful. There was no reason to pull forward anyway. There was no place to go. Palmer sat in his cab watching the ambulance attendants lay the body on a stretcher and cover it with a white sheet while the tow truck driver hooked up the vacant taxi.

He thought about quitting for the day, giving up his lease and going home, but he needed the money, always needed the money, and after the tow truck moved the veteran's cab out of the way, Palmer pulled forward to fill the slot, then realized that when he picked up the next passenger outside the front door of the terminal, he would be hauling the dead man's fare.

One morning in early April, as Palmer was checking the oil in his taxi, the morning-shift cashier came outside and told him that the previous driver had turned his cab in early with three dollars' worth of gas in it, and had asked that the next driver reimburse him for it. It was the sort of chickenshit nonsense that Palmer had come to expect from cab drivers, army chickenshit, so he did not argue but only smiled and dug out three dollars and handed it to the cashier. He always made a point never to hassle a cashier.

He got into his cab and headed out on the road feeling as though he had deposited a small token of good will into this cashier's account which would reap benefits in the future.

You do a favor for the cashier, he'll do a favor for you someday, maybe hold a cab for you on a morning when too many people want to drive, or forgive you small mistakes that he might not forgive another driver. Already he was thinking of this job in terms of the future. Enough time had passed with so few problems that he had come to realize that he could stay with this job forever if he absolutely had to. This was the best job he had ever held. Even though he cleared only sixty dollars on an average day, there was no supervisor standing over him, nothing was expected of him except the ability to drive. He did not even have to get a haircut, although the monthly newsletter gently reminded the drivers that good hygiene translated into good tips.

He drove to the Hilton, and after an hour a woman came out with a suitcase and got into his cab and said the magic word "Airport." Women tipped well. Young men of college age were terrible tippers. Waitresses tipped best, sometimes overtipped. This particular woman gave him fifteen dollars for a ten-dollar trip, and he laughed aloud only after he was headed for the airport cab line.

The April newsletter had come out, and after Palmer got parked he read through it and saw a small box printed on the second-to-last page, an obituary for the man who had died in the airport cab line one month earlier. His name was Edwin Mueller. He was sixty-eight years old. He was a veteran of World War Two. He had no family.

The cabs moved forward three spaces. When Palmer got to the terminal he picked up two men wearing suits who said they wanted to go to the Tech Center down south. They were from Chicago, were strangers to Denver, and the older of the two pulled out a yellow scrap of paper with instructions to take Interstate-25 which bisected the city. Palmer told him he knew of a shorter route, 225, which would be faster and cheaper. But the man was from Chicago, obviously did not trust cab drivers, and insisted they go by the route on the paper. Someone's secretary had given it to him over the phone.

Palmer made a last tepid effort to change the man's mind, then headed out. Halfway there the older of the two leaned forward and impatiently asked if they were getting close. Palmer told him they were halfway. He dropped them off in front of a building made of black glass. The two men split a fare of fifty-five dollars, including tip. Palmer offered both of them a receipt, a gesture that he learned could ameliorate the resentment of customers who felt they had somehow been cheated. This was the feeling he got from the Chicagoans, even though he had followed their instructions. They felt that somehow they had been cheated, and they were right. They had cheated themselves.

He stopped at a 7-Eleven for a Coke, feeling as if money was slipping through his fingers with this quick break. Take a piss, buy a pop, get back in the cab. Don't waste time out on the road, waste it in the airport line. This was one of many lessons he had learned during the past six months, like beating the day drivers to a cab on Friday morning, so many lessons learned that he could not remember having learned them, but was able now to drive with a minimum of mistakes. Remember to write down the mileage, turn in the vouchers, ignore the radio calls for desperate passengers too far across the city to help, and if a customer pays with a personal check, drive to his bank and cash it that day or live to regret it.

Palmer liked this job. He could no longer remember the last time he had sat reading want ads on a Sunday evening, glancing at listings for Editors, Technical Writers, vaguely considering the possibility of finding another white-collar job, but also looking at ads for truck drivers—shorter hours and better pay than cab driving, he supposed. But there would be a boss to answer to. Schedules to keep. Boxes to lift, to protect. It made him think of all the jobs he'd held that he had hated so much.

When Palmer was eighteen, a young Puerto Rican man had driven the furniture truck for a few months. They both liked to drink beer, they both hated the foreman, and they conspired to stay out on deliveries until a few minutes before the shop closed. At noon they would find a pizza parlor that sold 3.2 beer, and they would have as many as four beers apiece before getting back out on the road. They giggled and stumbled through their deliveries, hauling chairs and couches into the homes of lone women. The driver told Palmer stories about his youth in Puerto Rico, about giant rats that built nests in trees. When the man came to America he applied only for busboy jobs because that's all he knew how to do. Palmer was sorry to the see him quit after the boss had refused him a raise of twenty-five cents an hour.

The driver who replaced him was an alcoholic twenty-six-year-old who lasted barely a month. Every morning he bought a can of orange pop at a 7-Eleven and poured out half and filled it with vodka.

"I need it for my nerves," he would tell Palmer, who found this amusing. Palmer was a beer drinker. Hard liquor was as foreign to him as calculus. One afternoon they got into a minor accident involving the hidden branch of a tall tree which extended out over the road and dented the front of the cargo box above the cab. Even a sober driver would not have seen it, so Palmer found it ironic, and amusing in its way, like a scene in a movie, that the tippling truck driver had been the one chosen by fate to get ambushed.

On another occasion the same driver almost lost control of the truck while exiting Interstate-70. He violently jerked the steering wheel to keep it on the off-ramp, and only then did Palmer realize something dangerous had happened, yet he did not associate it with the vodka. Oblivious to reality throughout his youth, Palmer had felt cupped safely in the palm of God right up to the moment he arrived in Vietnam where he told himself that if he ever got home from Vietnam alive he would never complain about anything ever again. But it had been a hard promise to live up to.

When the cab line wasn't moving at the airport, when the sun was streaming through the windows of his cab generating a heat that made him drowsy, he thought about his past, thought about the twenty-four years that had gone by since he left home without his ever having accomplished anything he had wanted to accomplish when he was young. He thought about the fact that he still felt as if he was in his mid-twenties. He didn't feel forty-two years old. He didn't dress like he was forty-two years old. His father had worn a suit and a hat to work, had worn an overcoat on cold days. As a child Palmer would watch his father drive away in the family Buick, headed for his job, and he had wondered how he would dress when he grew up, what kind of suit he would wear, what kind of job he would be going to. He had tried to imagine himself as an adult, going to work in an overcoat and hat. He had wondered what was through the door of adulthood, as if it was waiting to embrace him and place him somewhere that he could not imagine but which he felt would be a much better place than childhood.

His memories of Vietnam were still vivid, but he could barely remember anything that had happened during the twenty years since then. College. Shit jobs. Girlfriends. Ambitions. Failures. Like one long meaningless day.

Now, in his contentment, Palmer no longer thought about his future. The thin but steady stream of money that passed through his hands to the apartment manager or grocery clerks had a lulling effect, in that as long as it kept flowing he would never have to worry about anything. He supposed he would be driving a cab for the rest of his life. What else could he do? It would take a career with exceptionally good pay to lure him away from dozing in the streaming sunlight at the airport in the afternoon while the steady buzz of cabbie conversations took place beyond his closed windows. It would take a job with outlandish benefits and quick promotions to make him give up the option of working or not working on any day of the week in any season of the year.

After he left the 7-Eleven that morning he drove downtown and parked outside the Hilton and began reading a paperback book. His was the only cab in line. It was a slow day. A few minutes later the rear door opened and a young and disheveled man got in, coatless, looked like the sort of person Palmer saw hanging around outside the Men's Mission. "Take me to Colfax and Broadway," the man said.

Palmer closed his paperback and turned around in his seat. "Colfax and Broadway is only two blocks over," he said,

trying to control the disgust that crept into his voice whenever an idiot got into his cab.

The man grinned at him and said, "Okay, take me up to
Capitol Hill."

It was a slow day. Palmer decided to go ahead and take
him. The fare would be two or three bucks. He turned on the
meter and pulled away from the curb. He drove over to
Broadway, turned up Colfax, and took his fare past the
Capitol building. As they rolled along Colfax, Palmer said,
"Where do you want to be let out?"

"I don't have any money," the man said.

Palmer glanced back at him. "What?"

"I don't have any money."

Palmer turned off the meter, pulled the cab over to the
curb and parked. He turned in his seat and said, "Get out."

The man didn't seem to be drunk, no tell-tale odor of
alcohol. He sat grinning at Palmer. "What do you mean?" he
said.

"I mean get out of my taxi."

"Just like that?" the man said, as though he had been
expecting a more interesting confrontation—a call to the
police department perhaps.

"Just like that," Palmer said.

The man shrugged and opened the door, climbed out and
closed it. Palmer drove back to the Hilton, doing his best to
project his thoughts into the future where this small incident
promised to be amusing.

He was third in line at the Hilton now, and could not help
but think about the fares to the airport that he would be
missing out on. The two cabbies ahead of him would drive

to Aspen. They would get rich. This was what he always thought after his place in a cab line had been screwed up.

As soon as he pulled up first in line, he saw a man cross the street against a red light up ahead and hurry down the sidewalk, and Palmer knew he was going to get into the cab. He didn't want this man, he wanted a fare from the hotel, a passenger going to the airport. He hated it when pedestrians with no luggage got into his cab. He knew this would not be an airport run.

The man leaned into the passenger window and said, "Listen, I need you to do something for me." He seemed rather panicked. Palmer set his paperback down and asked what he could do.

The man pointed up the block and said, "There's this old fellow on crutches standing in the doorway of a building about three blocks from here. He's a cripple. He can't get around by himself. I'll pay you ten dollars if you'll take him where he wants to go. He says he wants to go to the Tip-Top Inn on Fifteenth Street." As he spoke the man was digging through his billfold, explaining that the crippled man had begged for help, had asked him to find a cab.

Palmer took the ten dollars and got directions to the building. He pulled out of the cab line and drove three blocks and saw a large man standing in the doorway, coatless, leaning on crutches, wearing a shoe on one foot and a slipper on the other. He looked to be in his sixties. Hatless. Hair stringy, wispy, where it wasn't balding. His shirt half-buttoned, his bare belly exposed. Palmer was astonished by the man's wretched condition. Where did he come from? How did he get this far on his own?

Palmer parked at the curb and hurried around and opened the rear door. The man began saying thank you, thank you, then asked Palmer to help him into the backseat. The man must have weighed three hundred pounds. "I have a hard time sitting down," he said. "You'll have to take it easy. My hip is broken."

Palmer held the crutches while the man eased himself into the cab. Knew how to do it. Must spend all his life easing himself into cabs. His slipper fell off and landed in the gutter where a thin stream of water was flowing. Palmer quickly grabbed it out of the water, then saw the man's foot. It was a mass of bleeding sores. Where did this guy come from? Did he escape from a hospital? Palmer eased the slipper back onto the man's foot, then noting that he was having trouble twisting around to get settled on the seat, Palmer took his leg by the ankle and tried to maneuver it into the cab. The man began screaming with pain. It was a terrible scream, a woman's scream. "My hip! My hip!"

Palmer began to feel strange, as if he was standing outside himself. He felt helpless. The man lay down on the backseat to get his leg in. Palmer closed the door and hurried around to the driver's side. The Tip-Top was only six blocks away and he wanted to get this over with as quickly as possible.

He climbed in and started the engine, pulled out into traffic and inhaled an odor so foul that his lungs almost collapsed. It came from the man in the backseat, a smell unlike anything Palmer had ever encountered in his life, worse than skunk or shit or dead animal, the odor of a human body that hasn't been washed in months. Palmer's esophagus started to lurch uncontrollably. He was going to vomit. He rolled his window down and stuck his head out and began inhaling the breeze created by the motion of the cab, gulping fresh air. He kept his head outside the taxi all the way to the Tip-Top Inn.

During the brief moment of parking the cab the stink rolled over him again. He threw the door open and leaped out and stood there gasping and touching his stomach, afraid he might vomit right in the street.

He went around to the passenger side and opened the door. The fare seemed to know how to get out on his own, was good at it, grabbing the door and hauling himself to a standing position. "Thank you, thank you," the man said. Palmer reached into the backseat and retrieved the crutches. "Do you need help getting into the bar?" Palmer said.

"No," the man said. "If you can just help me up to the wall, I'll be all right."

Holding his breath, his lips clamped tight, Palmer took hold of the man's arm and escorted him to the wall.

"Are you sure you don't need help getting inside?" Palmer said, but the man shook his head no and said he was fine, he would be okay.

Palmer walked back to his cab, opened all the doors, and began rolling the windows all the way down. He shut the doors and got into the driver's seat and looked at the man leaning back against the wall. Did this man have friends in the bar? Was this his regular watering hole? Who would sit next to him? Who would help him home? Where did he live? What was wrong with his foot?

It would occur to Palmer later that he ought to have called the police, or at least an ambulance. But he only drove back to the Hilton.

★ ★ ★

Palmer woke up on a Friday morning filled with an unaccountable feeling of elation, a kind of eagerness not only to get out on the road and make some cash, but to return to this apartment, this place where he would be living as long as he drove a cab, maybe even as long as he lived. Fridays always made him feel good, made him feel prematurely rich. He cooked a breakfast of bacon and eggs and ate them in his aerie with the curtains drawn back so he could see the changing of the colors in the dawn, a thin line of pale blue at the curve of the earth as he ate his eggs, a wash of pink as he chewed his bacon, the Denver smog paling as he munched his blackened toast. This was his life, and he liked it.

He arrived at the cab company half an hour earlier than the rush of day drivers looking for a Friday score. There were twelve cabs available, and he took number 396, one of his favorites. Solid upholstery, you sat high on the seat, good acceleration, a clean cab, he checked the oil and water, then radioed the dispatcher who cleared him to go out on the road.

His first fare out of the Hilton went to the Tech Center, a fifteen-dollar trip. After he dropped the man off, he picked up two young businessmen whose deal seemed to have fallen through. They sat silently in the backseat with their briefcases on their laps. "I'll call Wilson when we get back," one said, and the other said nothing. Wilson was probably waiting to hear if the Carruthers deal had panned out. Big investment at stake. He would be disappointed. They sat silently in the backseat. They were the most forlorn businessmen Palmer had ever hauled in his cab, but they tipped well.

Young businessmen were his favorite customers, turks
with the facts and figures at their fingertips, men on the make
in their five-hundred-dollar suits and thirty-dollar haircuts,
well-bred, intelligent, articulate, even in conversations
with a cab driver they spoke as though they were making
a presentation at a meeting. They all seemed curious about
his work, curious to know what sort of person would settle
for taxi driving as a vocation, curious to know the gut details,
who makes these cabs, how much mileage do you put on one
in a year, do they still manufacture Checker cabs? Those
babies were indestructible. It was a treat to talk to junior
executives. Palmer imagined how easily they would finesse
him in business deals if he was one of their kind. Strategies,
stats, game plans, they thrived on the very things that
stumped Palmer.

Rather than park in the cab line and work the airport,
Palmer got on Interstate-70 which looped around the north
end of town and would bring him back to the hotels quickly.
As he was cruising along the highway the engine died and
came back to life, and in the brief moment that his body had
been thrust forward against his seatbelt, his heart skipped
a beat.

The cab continued moving, but Palmer could no longer
hear the firing of the pistons. He cranked the window down
and listened, heard only the whistle of polluted wind. Were
the pistons even functioning? He stepped on the accelerator
then lifted his foot, but it didn't seem to make any difference.
The cab was sailing along as if drawn by the gravity of the
far mountains. There was not much traffic, a few cars ahead
of him, a few behind, and if he needed to pull off onto the

shoulder of the highway he would have no problem. An exit ramp appeared a quarter mile further along and he decided he had better get off the highway altogether.

He tapped on the accelerator but there seemed no connection between the engine and his foot, his mind, his fear. He guided the coasting cab off the highway, aimed it down the ramp, an ancient steep concrete incline built back in the Fifties when highways were just beginning to demolish the Denver neighborhoods. He stepped on the brakes, but there were no brakes. The engine had died. No brakes, no steering, he was rolling down a steep slope inside a ton of steel over which he had no control, and there was an intersection ahead, a service highway that semi-tractor trailers used to circumvent the northern fringes of the city, the road blockaded only by the octagonal metal of a stop sign.

He gripped the steering wheel and threw his whole weight against it, yanked it to the left and managed to turn the wheels so that the left front tire began rubbing against the cement curb that bordered the ramp, slowing the cab and bringing it finally to a halt ten feet from the intersection.

Steam drifted from the grill. The engine had overheated. The radiator began spraying water, might have split at the seams, the entire engine must have locked up from a lack of coolant, pistons jamming inside the cylinders, shafts breaking off. Such luck. What if there had been a passenger in here, someone late for a plane?

The steam began to billow from the sides of the hood, and Palmer recalled something someone had told him about opening a hood to allow cool air to get to an overheated engine. He thought he ought to do that. Hop out and pop the hood and let the engine cool, then hike to a gas station across the highway for a can of water. Thoughts like these. But he only sat staring at the steam, which began to take on a brownish hue. Brown steam. He smelled it seeping in through the vents, and realized it was smoke. The engine was on fire.

He stared at the smoke coming from the front and sides of the hood, brown and boiling, pouring toward him like a breaking wave. It took a second for him to realize that he was in a bit of danger. Something not quite real about this. The smoke completely smothered the windshield, he couldn't see anything in front of him. He reached down quickly and gathered the trip sheet with the ballpoint pen clipped to it, the small leather briefcase that contained his maps and blank vouchers and receipts which he gave out to executives. There was a small metal box that contained a flashlight, small screwdrivers, Phillips and flathead, a pair of pliers, a plastic box containing change, silver and pennies. All of these he gathered up as the smoke seeped into the cab making him choke. He unsnapped his seatbelt and dove out.

There was a strip of land between the edge of the off-ramp and a chain-link fence, perhaps ten yards wide, and Palmer crossed this zone of safety and turned to look at the column of smoke rising into the sky. Beneath the engine tiny droplets of flame were hitting the ground. The engine was burning, everything combustible was melting, and it occurred to him that if he had gone ahead and opened the hood the sudden influx of oxygen could have created a ball of fire that might have burned his face, which was plausible only because it fit so perfectly into the schematic of his life.

The paint on the hood began to bubble, to turn black. It was the sight of the burning paint that made Palmer realize his job had come to an end. There would be no saving the cab.

He had managed to set it on fire, and the company would probably revoke his license, might even charge him for the damage. His job was over, the best job he ever had. Then a police cruiser entered the off-ramp going the wrong way and pulled up facing the flaming taxi. A policeman climbed out and hollered, "Are you all right?"

Palmer nodded. The cop sat back down in the driver's seat and lifted a microphone. A call to the fire department. Palmer looked at his cab. The paint was gone from the hood now, leaving only black scorched bare metal. The ground beneath the cab was a garden of flames. The fire had worked its way inside the cab, and Palmer moved closer and peered through the windows and saw that the front seat was on fire. The dashboard was melting. The padded steering wheel was a ring of fire. He walked over to the police car and waited until the cop had finished talking on the microphone.

When the cop got out, Palmer asked if there was any way the man could call the cab company and inform them that one of their cabs was on fire. The cop had a portable phone in his car, and he made the call. Before he hung up, a firetruck arrived with a dozen firefighters costumed in heavy yellow rubber coats and trousers and boots. Palmer expected them to leap from the truck and run to his cab with extinguishers at the ready while someone hooked a hose to a fireplug. But the firefighters moved about slowly as though they knew the inevitable outcome, knew that they were here only to see that the fire did not spread to the weeds that grew in the narrow strip of adjacent land where Palmer stood alone watching things take their various courses: policeman talking on the microphone; firefighters strolling about; taxi burning;

automobiles cautiously coming down the ramp and slowly passing the inferno.

The cop turned on his flashing red lights and drove slowly up the off-ramp to begin blocking any traffic that might try to come down. Emergency diversion. How much inconvenience is this going to cause total strangers, Palmer wondered as he gazed skyward and saw that the column of smoke was being pulled by a gentle wind across the highway overhead. Probably just enough to cause a few fender-benders. He expected a news truck from a TV station to pull up at any moment and begin taping the carnage. Taxicab burns. Traffic snarled for hours. Two people taken to local hospital for treatment of minor injuries. Stay tuned for an interview with the cab driver.

A firefighter began chopping at the grill with an axe, trying to get the hood open. Palmer wandered toward the safety of the cyclone fence and leaned back against it and watched as what appeared to be a high-ranking firefighter, a captain maybe, waved aside the man with the axe, reached under the front of the hood with a gloved hand, and undid the latch. He quickly raised the hood and stepped back. Ball of black smoke, oxygen at last free to roam the devastated landscape of the carburetor and radiator and spark-plugs, all the wiring now bare of rubber. The firefighters began spraying the engine with foam extinguishers as the flames crawled into the backseat and burrowed into the trunk. The cab's external paint job mapped the progress of the flames as it bubbled, smoked, and disappeared from hood to roof to trunk as though being sprayed by torches while passing through a car wash.

A shot, something like the sound of a small cannon, startled Palmer. He saw the right front corner of the car drop a few inches. The tire had exploded. During the next few minutes each of the remaining tires exploded like exclamation points on a pink slip that told Palmer he would have to begin looking for work somewhere else right away.

The firefighters continued to spray foam at the car, but did not make any actual effort to save it. What had once been a taxicab was now a shell resting on the road, black, devoid of paint and seats and tires and rubber mats. A tow truck contracted by the cab company showed up, and the driver began making preparations for the removal of the corpse. A firefighter approached Palmer with a question. He wanted to know the public utilities commission number which had been on the left rear fender but had been burned off. Palmer didn't know the number.

"Do you need my driver's license?" Palmer said, prepared to turn himself in to the authorities.

No, the firefighter didn't need it. Nobody else approached him to ask about the fire, about how it started, as though this sort of incident was routine and, barring personal injury, did not mean much. The firefighters climbed onto their truck, which pulled away leaving Palmer alone with the tow-truck driver who went about his quiet business of putting the body of the cab onto the rear flatbed of his vehicle and attaching hooks and chains to the scorched and gutted and useless piece of shit that had been Palmer's livelihood.

The light on the cop car continued to flash above on the ramp. The pall of smoke had faded, and no TV crews had shown up. When the driver finished chaining down the

wreckage, he told Palmer to hop into the tow truck for a ride
back to the cab company.

The quickest route back was to follow a service road that
ran directly beneath Interstate-70, which served as a viaduct
along this stretch, the highway a roof covering what in the
Fifties had been the main road leading to Stapleton Airport,
which had been called an airfield in the early days. Palmer
stared out the window at the approaching columns of concrete that held up the viaduct. He would have to find another
job quickly. It had been a mistake to rent the new apartment,
which was twice as expensive as the bunker where he had
lived after being thrown out by his last girlfriend. Time to
look for another job, and he realized that if he'd ever had it in
him to work alongside anyone or take orders from anyone
without feeling trapped and defeated, he would probably be
working toward a pension right now instead of towing a
piece of smoldering shit down an empty road.

The driver turned at an intersection and took them out
of the shadow of the viaduct, traveled along a street past
redbrick warehouse buildings and refineries, then turned
again and drove down a street that brought them to the front
entrance of the cab company. The driver braked, and smiled
for the first time at Palmer, and said, "You can hop out here.
I have to take your cab to the junkyard."

Palmer gathered his things and climbed down from the
tow truck and shut the door. He watched the truck pull away,
stared at the ruins of his cab which resembled the husk of a
dead locust. Then he went into the drivers' room and walked
up to the cashier.

"My cab burned up," he said.

The man grinned at him. "Yeah, we heard about that. The manager came running through here and said your cab blew up." The cashier laughed, then reached behind him and picked up a blank trip sheet. "You still got a couple hours left on your lease. Do you want another cab?"

Palmer nodded but didn't say anything. The cashier filled out the paperwork and handed over the keys to number 319, a cab that Palmer had driven before, a good cab.

Palmer stepped outside into the waning sunlight. That old familiar and capricious sense of unreality began to creep over him again. He roamed through the parking lot and found 319, got in, and without bothering to check the oil or water radioed the dispatcher and reported that he was back on the road.

He wrote his mileage down on the trip sheet, started the engine, drove out of the lot, and headed for Stapleton. He wanted to make one more run before the day was over, to confirm to himself that he had not lost his job, that he did not have to go back to his apartment that evening and do what he had done so many times in his life after losing jobs that he had hated: open the paper to the want ads. He could not remember ever having lost a job that he had liked.

The wind began to blow when he arrived at the airport, and by the time he was first in line at the chute the wind was so strong that the drivers who were huddled against the ramp wall began speculating as to whether or not incoming planes might be diverted to Dallas or Atlanta. One hundred mile an hour winds out of Boulder were reported on the radio. Dark clouds were coming in from the west. Palmer picked up a businessman who wanted to go to the Brown Palace. A ten-dollar trip and the man tipped two bucks.

Palmer turned his cab in after that and got into his heap and drove to his apartment under an unnaturally black sky, the heavy clouds obliterating the spring sunset. When he parked and got out, large drops of rain were hitting the ground like bird eggs knocked from tree branches swaying overhead in the stiff wind. He hurried up to his apartment and entered the kitchen, and looked out at the lights of the city which had come on early, as they had back in the wintertime, office buildings, streetlights, headlights, the casual defense of a citizenry used to Colorado weather.

He took off his coat and sat down at the kitchen table. He parted a curtain on a window and studied the storm, pondered its curious fury, and listened to the lesser winds that whistled in the burgeoning lulls. Wet leaves tumbled out of the darkness, slapped flat against the windows, clung trembling to the glass, were peeled off by the wind and tossed into the night. Two hours ago he had envisioned himself seated at this table, gazing at the classified section of the newspaper and hoping that a line of black print would leap out at him promising a job that he knew in his heart that he could do because he had to. Now he sat motionless at the kitchen table feeling an odd loss of momentum, the sensation that he ought to be doing something he had expected to be doing: turning the large leaves of the *Denver Post* with a ballpoint pen clamped between his fingers. Both his mind and his body had been braced for this small though onerous effort, and now that he no longer had it to do, he felt edgy, off-balance, like a sailor in dry-dock fighting the vertigo of nonexistent waves. He could not recall any time in recent memory when there was nothing that he had to do. When everything was okay. When he was safe.

He sat at the table until the darkness outside matched the darkness inside his crow's nest, then he stood up from the table and turned on the kitchen light. Maybe he would take up writing again.

The End

CPSIA information can be obtained
at www.ICGtesting.com
Printed in the USA
FSOW01n2206140617
35237FS